PENGUIN C

BRODIE'S RE

JORGE LUIS BORGES was born in Buenos Aires in 1899 and was educated in Europe. One of the most widely acclaimed writers of our time, he published many collections of poems, essays, and short stories before his death in Geneva in June 1986. In 1961 Borges shared the International Publisher's Prize with Samuel Beckett. The Ingram Merrill Foundation granted him its Annual Literary Award in 1966 for his "outstanding contribution to literature." In 1971 Columbia University awarded him the first of many degrees of Doctor of Letters, *honoris causa* (eventually the list included both Oxford and Cambridge), that he was to receive from the English-speaking world. In 1971 he also received the fifth biennial Jerusalem Prize and in 1973 was given one of Mexico's most prestigious cultural awards, the Alfonso Reyes Prize. In 1980 he shared with Gerardo Diego the Cervantes Prize, the Spanish world's highest literary accolade. Borges was Director of the Argentine National Library from 1955 until 1973.

ANDREW HURLEY is Professor of English at the University of Puerto Rico in San Juan, where he also teaches in the Translation Program. He has translated over two dozen book-length works of history, poetry, and fiction, including novels by Reinaldo Arenas, Ernesto Sabato, Fernando Arrabal, Gustavo Sainz, and Edgardo Rodríguez Juliá and sotries by Ana Lydia Vega, and many shorter works.

JORGE LUIS BORGES

Brodie's Report

INCLUDING THE PROSE FICTION FROM
IN PRAISE OF DARKNESS

Translated with an Introduction by
ANDREW HURLEY

PENGUIN BOOKS

PENGUIN BOOKS

Published by the Penguin Group
Penguin Group (USA) Inc., 375 Hudson Street, New York, New York 10014, U.S.A.
Penguin Group (Canada), 90 Eglinton Avenue East, Suite 700, Toronto, Ontario,
Canada MP4 2Y3 (a division of Pearson Penguin Canada Inc.)
Penguin Books Ltd, 80 Strand, London WC2R 0RL, England
Penguin Ireland, 25 St Stephen's Green, Dublin 2, Ireland (a division of Penguin Books Ltd)
Penguin Group (Australia), 250 Camberwell Road, Camberwell, Victoria 3124, Australia
(a division of Pearson Australia Group Pty Ltd)
Penguin Books India Pvt Ltd, 11 Community Centre, Panchsheel Park, New Delhi – 110 017, India
Penguin Group (NZ), cnr Airborne and Rosedale Roads, Albany, Auckland 1310, New Zealand
(a division of Pearson New Zealand Ltd)
Penguin Books (South Africa) (Pty) Ltd, 24 Sturdee Avenue, Rosebank, Johannesburg 2196, South Africa

Penguin Books Ltd, Registered Offices:
80 Strand, London WC2R 0RL, England

These translations first published in *Collected Fictions* in the USA by Viking Penguin,
a member of Penguin Putnam Inc. 1998
First published in Great Britain by Allen Lane The Penguin Press 1999
Published in Penguin Books UK 2000
Published in Penguin Books USA 2005

1 3 5 7 9 10 8 6 4 2

This selection was originally published by Emece Editores, Buenos Aires,
as the collection *El informe de Brodie*

THE LIBRARY OF CONGRESS HAS CATALOGED THIS EDITION AS FOLLOWS:
Borges, Jorge Luis, 1899–
[Informe de Brodie. English]
Brodie's report : including the prose fiction from In praise of darkness / Jorge Luis Borges ;
translated with an introduction by Andrew Hurley.
p. cm.
ISBN 0 14 30.3925 3
I. Hurley, Andrew.   II. Borges, Jorge Luis, 1899– Elogio de la sombra. English. Selections.
III. Title: In praise of darkness.   IV. Title.
PQ7797.B6351513 2005
863'.62—dc22   2005045806

Printed in the United States of America

Contents

Introduction

After a period of twenty years in which Borges had published no short stories or tales and almost ten years in which he had published very little prose fiction of any kind—in which, in fact, he seems to have convinced himself that he would never write prose fiction again—suddenly, in 1969 and 1970, he began not just writing it again, but almost churning it out. In August of 1969, to coincide with his seventieth birthday, Borges published a volume of poems and prose fictions titled *In Praise of Darkness (Elogio de la sombra)*; a year later, he followed that collection with another, composed exclusively of short stories, titled *Brodie's Report (El informe de Brodie)*. This torrent of publications in such a short time was almost unprecedented in Borges' career, and especially remarkable after such a long drought.

Unlike Borges' usual practice for collections of his prose or poetry (bringing out many of the individual pieces in periodicals during the months leading up to the volume's publication), the five prose fictions in *In Praise of Darkness* had not been published previously; they were seeing the light of day for the first time in this volume. For the stories making up *Brodie's Report*, though, Borges' publishing practice reverted to form: on October 5, 1969, bare weeks after the publication of *In Praise of Darkness*, a story called "The Encounter" appeared in the Sunday supplement to the newspaper *La Prensa*, to celebrate the paper's hundredth anniversary; on November 9, "The Story from Rosendo Juárez" appeared in *La Nación*, where over the years so many of Borges' stories and poems had first been published. In March of the following year, "Juan Muraña" came out in *La Prensa*; in August, in *La Nación*, "The Gospel According to Mark." That same month, a Borges story, "The Other Duel," appeared in a venue new to him, a magazine titled *Los Libros*. Then, when that very month the full volume called *Brodie's Report* came out, readers discovered that Borges had added to these five stories a sixth, "The Interloper," which he had dictated to his mother and published in a small private edition in 1966, and five new stories never before published in periodicals: "Unworthy," "The Elderly Lady," "Guayaquil," "The Duel," and "Brodie's Report."[1]

In terms of genre, the pieces in *In Praise of Darkness* are something of a mixed bag: "Pedro Salvadores" and "The Ethnographer" (whose name over the course of subsequent years and editions Borges changed from "The Ethnographer" to "The Ethnologist" and back again) are clearly "short stories" as that term is generally understood (though still having something of the parable about them), while one might reasonably call "His End and His Beginning" a prose-poetic "reflection" or "meditation," and Nicolás Helft, in his recent exhaustive bibliography of Borges' publications, goes so far as to consider "A Legend" and "A Prayer" to be "poems." (In that, the present translator disagrees, but then that genre-ambiguity is precisely the point.) The miscellaneousness extends into the stories' themes: in their concern with time and human life and death, and in their questioning of the existence (and desirability) of an afterlife, the last three fictions named above look back to the prose-poems of *The Maker* while clearly reflecting the natural concerns of an old man, Borges at seventy, who is aware that his life is running out. But countering

1. For the precise publishing information contained here, I wish most gratefully to acknowledge the important bibliographical work done by Nicolás Helft and published in *Jorge Luis Borges: Bibliografía completa* (Mexico City/Buenos Aires: Fondo de Cultura Económica, 1997).

this "old man" theory of the fictions is that remarkable story "Pedro Salvadores," which looks not only backward to earlier stories, earlier books, earlier obsessions, but forward as well, as we see now in retrospect, to the themes that pervade *Brodie's Report.*

There are so many things about "Pedro Salvadores" that make it not just "Borgesian" but also pivotal, in an almost architectural sense, between the past and future of Borges' career: first, it is a story like so many others that come to mind—"The Disinterested Killer Bill Harrigan," "The Shape of the Sword," "The Garden of Forking Paths," "Story of the Warrior and the Captive Maiden," "A Biography of Tadeo Isidoro Cruz," "The Wait," "Emma Zunz," "Averroës' Search," "*Deutsches Requiem*," "The Captive," "Covered Mirrors," "Avelino Arredondo," and more— in which Borges confronts the reader with the mystery of a person's mind, the mystery of a person's motivation for an act which, seen as it must be from the "outside," is literally incomprehensible. That confrontation with the human (not metaphysical or theological) Unknown, or Unknowable, was one of Borges' most constant themes, and here, as in many of those other stories, it has been woven into an ambiguous parable of fear or courage. Then "Pedro Salvadores" is also a story about Argentine history, and while it looks backward to some of Borges' best poetry and many prose reflections, it also looks forward (did Borges know he was about to plunge once again into the history of the region?) to several stories in *Brodie's Report* and *The Book of Sand*—"The Elderly Lady," "Guayaquil," "Avelino Arredondo." But the aspect of this story that readers can now, with the advantage of retrospect, see as most telling of all is the fearsome and brutal violence that drives the plot.

Early in his career, Borges had written books filled with, almost obsessed by, violence; of those first years one thinks especially of *A Universal History of Iniquity* and the biography *Evaristo Carriego*. *A Universal History of Iniquity* was about just that—iniquity;

Carriego was not merely about a minor Buenos Aires poet, it was also about old Buenos Aires itself, its tough neighborhoods, its tangos, its knife fighters, and its streetcorners. But beyond those early years and fascinations, the reader who, on down through the years, expected a Borges story to be an epicene and metaphysical meditation would have deserved to be shocked at the violence and brutality that run through, and in fact propel, the stories. One after another, the stories present scenes of murder (both cold-blooded and hot-blooded), throat-slitting, political assassination, political and personal betrayal, mob betrayal (there is no honor among thieves in Borges—look at "Unworthy" and "The Dead Man"), armed robbery, knife fights, duels, bloodthirsty revenge, war, bloody conquest and destruction . . . (the list goes on and on). But since the stories collected in *The Aleph* in 1949, Borges had largely put this motif aside; *The Maker* (1960) is almost entirely about poetry and the imagination, not violence and bloodshed. With *Brodie's Report*, however, the violence appears again—and with, as they say, a vengeance. In fact, the book's secret title might well be "The Book of the Violent Argentine Past," or even "The Book of the Knife"—one of Borges' biographers, James Woodall, has quite rightly noted that Borges had not been "so visceral" since *A Universal History of Iniquity*. Two or three examples of the many possible: in "The Interloper" a brother cold-bloodedly kills a woman; the justification for the murder (which is really not seen as murder at all) has to do with the pampas (the *frontier*) cult of masculinity that declares that "any man who thinks five minutes about a woman is no man at all; he's a pansy." In "Unworthy," thieves are betrayed by one of their gang, a "good" young man, and then shot to death in cold blood by the police. In "Juan Muraña," "The Encounter," "The Story from Rosendo Juárez," and "The Other Duel," a knife (of the kind used in that peculiar Argentine ballet, the knife fight to the death) is used, once again in pure cold blood, to kill, and that is the entire "motor" of the plot. Thus, the threat of assassination in

"Pedro Salvadores" both recalls the past and foreshadows the future of Borges' thematic concern with violence.

There are no doubt several reasons for the persistence of this motif throughout Borges' career and its resurgence at this time. For one thing, it is clear that Borges (influenced perhaps by the movies, perhaps by the cult of the knife in old-time Buenos Aires) was fascinated by what might be called the aesthetics of violence; one of the pieces in *A Universal History of Iniquity* begins with the "dance" of a knife fight, the "tango" that brings two nattily dressed men together for this abstract, cinematic, and oddly erotic scene of death. For another, there is the element of "realism" in many of Borges' stories. We know—he told us over and over—that he was not "interested" in realism, that it was just one more literary convention, that he could "fake it" whenever he wanted to, and yet there is no doubt that Borges' stories often have a verisimilitude, a definiteness, a specificity of time and place that make them almost documentary chronicles of a moment in time, snapshots of a moment in the history of a city and a country—and that history was a violent one, as Borges also tells us. (On one side, he reminds us, his was a military family; he also reminds us that he had grown up in the neighborhood of Palermo in old Buenos Aires, where knife fights were not simply common, they were the accepted norm.) Associated with this verisimilitude may be a resignation in the face of "the facts," a sense that "life is like that," that violence had been and continued to be the fundamental, perhaps essential, way that humans solved their problems, that it underlay (as we see in "The Duel" in *Brodie's Report*) even the apparently trivial rivalry between two female and decidedly lady-like painters.

A "higher" (and ethically more palatable) reason for the constant motif of violence might be that however much Borges declawed and even glamorized violence by aestheticizing it, he clearly perceived its essential stupidity and brutality ("*bruto*" in Spanish means both bestial and stupid) and, by making violence so central to his stories, was offering a critique of his society—indeed of all humanity, for down through his career the stories ranged over all times and places. This ethical reason for the pervading violence of the stories is often overlooked, especially by those who see Borges as an aloof and mandarin writer disconnected from "social issues," but if we glance at stories such as "*Deutsches Requiem*" in *The Aleph* or "The Other Duel" and "The Interloper" in this volume, we see Borges the social critic offering a devastating critique of dehumanized and dehumanizing violence. This view may explain the choice of "Brodie's Report" as the story that gives its name to the volume it resides in: surely the "remedy" that Brodie's report *almost* suggests—the extermination or other "forced conversion" of a people who have a culture, a king, an architecture, a belief in the afterlife, a language very much like Arabic, and a patriotism that leads them to war, just like us—is one that he, Borges, found appalling. Like Defoe's *The Shortest Way with the Dissenters* and Swift's *Modest Proposal*, though, "Brodie's Report" never tips its hand, never preaches, never moralizes, never overtly notes that it is a cautionary fiction and a satire, not a horrific "modest proposal" at all. (And so it, like those other works, has run the risk of being misread all these years.) Borges' fascination with violence was surely in part a fascination with the horrendous, a fascination with that which is most physically nauseating and morally repugnant, and here, at what he thought was the end of his life (for he could not have known that he had another sixteen years to live), we can surely see Borges making his most powerful statement in decades on the waste and sickness of human violence.

But let us not stress one reading of these compelling stories over another. The fact is that as in all of Borges' work, there are many themes here—fate versus free will, magic, memory, subjectivity versus objective "truth," circular versus linear time (and thus East versus West, the forms of cosmology), friendship and comradeship and their variations, personal loyalty, human ethics, and storytelling itself, if not others besides—and many ways to read them. That word "compelling," though, cannot be denied. Especially in *Brodie's Report*, Borges achieved some of the most memorable and provocative stories of his long career, worthy to stand with the perhaps more famous stories of *Fictions* and *The Aleph* as high-order achievements of the writer's craft and art. But then as Borges himself self-deprecatingly (as always) noted in his Foreword to *Brodie*, surely what Kipling, a young man of genius, was able to do in *Plain Tales from the Hills*, a "man who was beginning to get along in years and who knows his craft" might also manage.

Andrew Hurley
San Juan, Puerto Rico
January 2000

In Praise of Darkness
(1969)

Foreword

Without realizing at first that I was doing so, I have devoted my long life to literature, teaching, idleness, the quiet adventures of conversation, philology (which I know very little about), the mysterious habit of Buenos Aires, and the perplexities which not without some arrogance are called metaphysics. Nor has my life been without its friendships, which are what really matter. I don't believe I have a single enemy—if I do, nobody ever told me. The truth is that no one can hurt us except the people we love. Now, at my seventy years of age (the phrase is Whitman's), I send to the press this fifth book of verse.

Carlos Frías has suggested that I take advantage of the foreword to this book to declare my æsthetics. My poverty, my will, resist that suggestion. I do not *have* an æsthetics. Time has taught me a few tricks—avoiding synonyms, the drawback to which is that they suggest imaginary differences; avoiding Hispanicisms, Argentinisms, archaisms, and neologisms; using everyday words rather than shocking ones; inserting circumstantial details, which are now demanded by readers, into my stories; feigning a slight uncertainty, since even though reality is precise, memory isn't; narrating events (this I learned from Kipling and the Icelandic sagas) as though I didn't fully understand them; remembering that tradition, conventions, "the rules," are not an obligation, and that time will surely repeal them—but such tricks (or habits) are most certainly not an æsthetics. Anyway, I don't believe in those formulations that people call "an æsthetics." As a general rule, they are no more than useless abstractions; they vary from author to author and even from text to text, and can never be more than occasional stimuli or tools.

This, as I said, is my fifth book of poetry. It is reasonable to assume that it will be no better or worse than the others. To the mirrors, labyrinths, and swords that my resigned reader will already have been prepared for have been added two new subjects: old age and ethics. Ethics, as we all know, was a constant preoccupation of a certain dear friend that literature brought me, Robert Louis Stevenson. One of the virtues that make me prefer Protestant nations to Catholic ones is their concern for ethics. Milton tried to educate the children in his academy in the knowledge of physics, mathematics, astronomy, and natural sciences; in the mid-seventeenth century Dr. Johnson was to observe that "Prudence and justice are preeminences and virtues which belong to all times and all places; we are perpetually moralists and only sometimes geometers."

In these pages the forms of prose and verse coexist, I believe, without discord. I might cite illustrious antecedents—Boethius' *Consolation of Philosophy*, Chaucer's *Tales,* the *Book of the Thousand Nights and a Night*; I prefer to say that those divergences look to me to be accidental—I hope this book will be read as a book of verse. A volume, *per se*, is not an aesthetic moment, it is one physical object among many; the aesthetic moment can only occur when the volume is written or read. One often hears that free verse is simply a typographical sham; I think there's a basic error in that statement. Beyond the rhythm of a line of verse, its typographical arrangement serves to tell the reader that it's poetic emotion, not information or rationality, that he or she should expect. I once yearned after the long breath line of the Psalms[1]

---

[1]. In the Spanish version of this Foreword, I deliberately spelled the word with its initial *p*, which is reprobated by most Peninsular grammarians. The members of the Spanish Royal Academy want to impose their own phonetic inabilities on the New World; they suggest such provincial forms as *neuma* for *pneuma*, *sicología* for *psicología*, and *síquico* for *psíquico*. They've even taken to prescribing *vikingo* for *viking*. I have a feeling we'll soon be hearing talk of the works of *Kiplingo*.

or Walt Whitman; after all these years I now see, a bit melancholically, that I have done no more than alternate between one and another classical meter: the alexandrine, the hendecasyllable, the heptasyllable.

In a certain *milonga* I have attempted, respectfully, to imitate the florid valor of Ascasubi* and the *coplas* of the barrios.

Poetry is no less mysterious than the other elements of the orb. A lucky line here and there should not make us think any higher of ourselves, for such lines are the gift of Chance or the Spirit; only the errors are our own. I hope the reader may find in my pages something that merits being remembered; in this world, beauty is so common.

J.L.B.
Buenos Aires, June 24, 1969

The Ethnographer

I was told about the case in Texas, but it had happened in another state. It has a single protagonist (though in every story there are thousands of protagonists, visible and invisible, alive and dead). The man's name, I believe, was Fred Murdock. He was tall, as Americans are; his hair was neither blond nor dark, his features were sharp, and he spoke very little. There was nothing singular about him, not even that feigned singularity that young men affect. He was naturally respectful, and he distrusted neither books nor the men and women who write them. He was at that age when a man doesn't yet know who he is, and so is ready to throw himself into whatever chance puts in his way—Persian mysticism or the unknown origins of Hungarian, algebra or the hazards of war, Puritanism or orgy. At the university, an adviser had interested him in Amerindian languages. Certain esoteric rites still survived in certain tribes out West; one of his professors, an older man, suggested that he go live on a reservation, observe the rites, and discover the secret revealed by the medicine men to the initiates. When he came back, he would have his dissertation, and the university authorities would see that it was published.

Murdock leaped at the suggestion. One of his ancestors had died in the frontier wars; that bygone conflict of his race was now a link. He must have foreseen the difficulties that lay ahead for him; he would have to convince the red men to accept him as one of their own. He set out upon the long adventure. He lived for more than two years on the prairie, sometimes sheltered by adobe walls and sometimes in the open. He rose before dawn, went to bed at sundown, and came to dream in a language that was not that of his fathers. He conditioned his palate to harsh flavors, he covered himself with strange clothing, he forgot his friends and the city, he came to think in a fashion that the logic of his mind rejected. During the first few months of his new education he secretly took notes; later, he tore the notes up—perhaps to avoid drawing suspicion upon himself, perhaps because he no longer needed them. After a period of time (determined upon in advance by certain practices, both spiritual and physical), the priest instructed Murdock to start remembering his dreams, and to recount them to him at daybreak each morning. The young man found that on nights of the full moon he dreamed of buffalo. He reported these recurrent dreams to his teacher; the teacher at last revealed to him the tribe's secret doctrine. One morning, without saying a word to anyone, Murdock left.

In the city, he was homesick for those first evenings on the prairie when, long ago, he had been homesick for the city. He made his way to his professor's office and told him that he knew the secret, but had resolved not to reveal it.

"Are you bound by your oath?" the professor asked.

"That's not the reason," Murdock replied. "I learned something out there that I can't express."

"The English language may not be able to communicate it," the professor suggested.

"That's not it, sir. Now that I possess the secret, I could tell it in a hundred different and even contradictory ways. I don't know how to tell you this, but the secret is beautiful, and science, *our* science, seems mere frivolity to me now."

After a pause he added:

"And anyway, the secret is not as important as the paths that led me to it. Each person has to walk those paths himself."

The professor spoke coldly:

"I will inform the committee of your decision. Are you planning to live among the Indians?"

"No," Murdock answered. "I may not even go back to the prairie. What the men of the prairie taught me is good anywhere and for any circumstances."

That was the essence of their conversation.

Fred married, divorced, and is now one of the librarians at Yale.

Pedro Salvadores

I want to put in writing, perhaps for the first time, one of the strangest and saddest events in the history of my country. The best way to go about it, I believe, is to keep my own part in the telling of the story small, and to suppress all picturesque additions and speculative conjectures.

A man, a woman, and the vast shadow of a dictator* are the story's three protagonists. The man's name was Pedro Salvadores; my grandfather Acevedo was a witness to his existence, a few days or weeks after the Battle of Monte Caseros.* There may have been no real difference between Pedro Salvadores and the common run of mankind, but his fate, the years of it, made him unique. He was a gentleman much like the other gentlemen of his day, with a place in the city and some land (we may imagine) in the country; he was a member of the Unitarian party.* His wife's maiden name was Planes; they lived together on Calle Suipacha, not far from the corner of Temple.* The house in which the events took place was much like the others on the street: the front door, the vestibule, the inner door, the rooms, the shadowy depth of the patios. One night in 1842, Pedro Salvadores and his wife heard the dull sound of hoofbeats coming closer and closer up the dusty street, and the wild huzzahs and imprecations of the horses' riders. But this time the horsemen of the tyrant's posse* did not pass them by. The whooping and shouting became insistent banging on the door. Then, as the men were breaking down the door, Salvadores managed to push the dining table to

9

one side, lift the rug, and hide himself in the cellar. His wife moved the table back into place. The posse burst into the house; they had come to get Salvadores. His wife told them he'd fled— to Montevideo, she told them. They didn't believe her; they lashed her with their whips, smashed all the sky blue china,* and searched the house, but it never occurred to them to lift the rug. They left at midnight, vowing to return.

It is at this point that the story of Pedro Salvadores truly begins. He lived in that cellar for nine years. No matter how often we tell ourselves that years are made of days, and days of hours, and that nine years is an abstraction, an impossible sum, the story still horrifies and appalls. I suspect that in the darkness that his eyes learned to fathom, he came not to think of anything—not even his hatred or his danger. He was simply there, in the cellar. Now and again, echoes of that world he could not enter would reach him from above: his wife's footsteps as she went about her routine, the thump of the water pump and the pail, the pelting of rain in the patio. Every day, too, might be his last.

His wife gradually got rid of all the servants; they were capable of informing on them. She told her family that her husband was in Uruguay. She earned a living for the two of them by sewing for the army. In the course of time she had two children; her family, attributing the children to a lover, repudiated her. After the fall of the tyrant they got down on their knees to her and begged forgiveness.

What, who, was Pedro Salvadores? Was he imprisoned by terror, love, the invisible presence of Buenos Aires, or, in the final analysis, habit? To keep him from leaving her, his wife would give him vague news of conspiracies and victories. Perhaps he was a coward, and his wife faithfully hid from him that she knew that. I picture him in his cellar, perhaps without even an oil lamp, or a book. The darkness would draw him under, into sleep. He would dream, at first, of the dreadful night when the knife would seek the throat, or dream of open streets, or of the plains. Within a few years, he would be incapable of fleeing, and he would dream of the cellar. At first he was a hunted man, a man in danger; later . . . we will never know—a quiet animal in its burrows, or some sort of obscure deity?

All this, until that summer day in 1852 when the dictator Rosas fled the country. It was then that the secret man emerged into the light of day; my grandfather actually spoke with him. Puffy, slack-muscled, and obese, Pedro Salvadores was the color of wax, and he spoke in a faint whisper. The government had confiscated his land; it was never returned to him. I believe he died in poverty.

We see the fate of Pedro Salvadores, like all things, as a symbol of something that we are just on the verge of understanding. . . .

Legend

Cain and Abel came upon each other after Abel's death. They were walking through the desert, and they recognized each other from afar, since both men were very tall. The two brothers sat on the ground, made a fire, and ate. They sat silently, as weary people do when dusk begins to fall. In the sky, a star glimmered, though it had not yet been given a name. In the light of the fire, Cain saw that Abel's forehead bore the mark of the stone, and he dropped the bread he was about to carry to his mouth and asked his brother to forgive him.

"Was it you that killed me, or did I kill you?" Abel answered. "I don't remember anymore; here we are, together, like before."

"Now I know that you have truly forgiven me," Cain said, "because forgetting is forgiving. I, too, will try to forget."

"Yes," said Abel slowly. "So long as remorse lasts, guilt lasts."

A Prayer

Thousands of times, and in both of the languages that are a part of me, my lips have pronounced, and shall go on pronouncing, the Paternoster, yet I only partly understand it. This morning— July 1, 1969—I want to attempt a prayer that is personal, not inherited. I know that such an undertaking demands a sincerity that is more than human. First of all, obviously I am barred from asking for anything. Asking that my eyes not be filled with night would be madness; I know of thousands of people who can see, yet who are not particularly happy, just, or wise. Time's march is a web of causes and effects, and asking for any gift of mercy, however tiny it might be, is to ask that a link be broken in that web of iron, ask that it be *already* broken. No one deserves such a miracle. Nor can I plead that my trespasses be forgiven; forgiveness is the act of another, and only I myself can save me. Forgiveness purifies the offended party, not the offender, who is virtually untouched by it. The freeness of my "free will" is perhaps illusory, but I am able to give, or to dream that I give. I can give courage, which I do not possess; I can give hope, which does not lie within me; I can teach a willingness to learn that which I hardly know myself, or merely glimpse. I want to be remembered less as poet than as friend; I want someone to repeat a cadence from Dunbar or Frost or that man who, at midnight, looked upon that tree that bleeds, the Cross, and to reflect that he heard those words for the first time from my lips. None of the rest matters to me; I hope that oblivion will not long delay. The designs of the universe are unknown to us, but we do know that to think with lucidity and to act with fairness is to aid those designs (which shall never be revealed to us).

I want to die completely; I want to die with this body, my companion.

His End and His Beginning

The death throes done, he lay now alone—alone and broken and rejected—and then he sank into sleep. When he awoke, there awaited him his commonplace habits and the places of his everyday existence. He told himself that he shouldn't think too much about the night before, and, cheered by that resolve, he unhurriedly dressed for work. At the office, he got through his duties passably well, though with that uneasy sense (caused by weariness) of repeating things he'd already done. He seemed to notice that the others turned their eyes away; perhaps they already knew that he was dead. That night the nightmares began; he was left without the slightest memory of them—just the fear that they'd return. In time, that fear prevailed; it came between him and the page he was supposed to write, the books he tried to read. Letters would crawl about on the page like ants; faces, familiar faces, gradually blurred and faded, objects and people slowly abandoned him. His mind seized upon those changing shapes in a frenzy of tenacity.

However odd it may seem, he never suspected the truth; it burst upon him suddenly. He realized that he was unable to remember the shapes, sounds, and colors of his dreams; there were no shapes, colors, or sounds, nor were the dreams dreams. They were his reality, a reality beyond silence and sight, and therefore beyond memory. This realization threw him into even greater consternation than the fact that from the hour of his death he had been struggling in a whirlwind of senseless images. The voices he'd heard had been echoes; the faces he'd seen had been masks; the fingers of his hands had been shadows—vague and insubstantial, true, yet also dear to him, and familiar.

Somehow he sensed that it was his duty to leave all these things behind; now he belonged to this new world, removed from past, present, and future. Little by little this new world surrounded him. He suffered many agonies, journeyed through realms of desperation and loneliness—appalling peregrinations for they transcended all his previous perceptions, memories, and hopes. All horror lay in their newness and their splendor. He had deserved grace—he had earned it; every second since the moment of his death, he had been in heaven.

Brodie's Report
(1970)

read some

Foreword

Kipling's last stories were no less tortured and labyrinthine than Franz Kafka's or Henry James's, which they unquestionably surpass; in 1885, though, in Lahore, early in his career, Kipling began writing a series of brief tales composed in a plain style, and he published those stories in 1890. Not a few of them—"In the House of Suddhoo,"* "Beyond the Pale," "The Gate of the Hundred Sorrows"—are laconic masterpieces; it has occurred to me from time to time that that which a young man of genius is capable of conceiving and bringing to fruition, a man beginning to get along in years and who knows his craft might, without immodesty, himself attempt. The issue of that reflection is contained in this volume; my readers may judge it for themselves.

I have tried (I am not sure how successfully) to write plain tales. I dare not say they are simple; there is not a simple page, a simple word, on earth—for all pages, all words, predicate the universe, whose most notorious attribute is its complexity. But I do wish to make clear that I am not, nor have I ever been, what used to be called a fabulist or spinner of parables, what these days is called an *auteur engagé*. I do not aspire to be Æsop. My tales, like those of the *Thousand and One Nights*, are intended not to persuade readers, but to entertain and touch them. This intention does not mean that I shut myself, as Solomon's image would have it, into an ivory tower. My convictions with respect to political matters are well known; I have joined the Conservative Party (which act is a form of skepticism), and no one has ever called me a Communist, a nationalist, an anti-Semite, or a supporter of Hormiga Negra* or of Rosas.* I believe that in time we will have reached the point where we will deserve to be free of government. I have never hidden my opinions, even through the difficult years, but I have never allowed them to intrude upon my literary production, either, save that one time when I praised the Six-Day War. The craft is mysterious; our opinions are ephemeral, and I prefer* Plato's theory of the Muse to that of Poe, who argued, or pretended to argue, that the writing of a poem is an operation of the intelligence. (I never cease to be amazed that the Classics professed a Romantic theory while a Romantic poet espoused a Classical one.)

Aside from the text that gives its name to this book (and whose paternity, obviously, can be traced to Lemuel Gulliver's last voyage), my stories are "realistic," to use a term that is fashionable these days. They observe, I believe, all the conventions of the genre (a genre no less convention-ridden than all the others, and one we will soon enough grow tired of, if we are not already). They abound in the circumstantial details that writers are required to invent—details that we can find such splendid examples of in the tenth-century Anglo-Saxon ballad of the Battle of Maldon and the Icelandic sagas that came later. Two of the stories (I will not say which ones) can be opened with the same fantastic key. The curious reader will perceive certain secret affinities among the tales. A mere handful of arguments have haunted me all these years; I am decidedly monotonous.

For the general outline of the story called "The Gospel According to Mark," the best story of the volume, I am indebted to a dream that Hugo Ramírez Moroni* had one night; I fear I may have spoiled the dream with the changes that my imagination (or my reason) deemed it needed. But then literature is naught but guided dreaming, anyway.

I have renounced the shocks of a baroque style as well as those afforded by unforeseen or unexpected endings. I have, in short, preferred to prepare my readers for my endings, rather than to astound them. For many years I believed that it would be my fortune to achieve literature through variations and novelties; now that I am seventy years old I think I have found my own voice. A word changed here or there will neither spoil nor improve what I dictate, except when those alterations succeed in leavening a heavy sentence or softening an emphasis. Each language is a tradition, each word a shared symbol; the changes that an innovator may make are trifling—we should remember the dazzling but often unreadable work of a Mallarmé or a Joyce. These reasonable, rational arguments are quite likely the result of weariness; advanced age has taught me to resign myself to being Borges.

I care little about the Diccionario de la Real Academia (*"dont chaque édition fait regretter la précédente,"* as Paul Grossac glumly remarked), and equally little about these tiresome dictionaries of Argentinisms. All of them—on both this side of the Atlantic and the other—tend to stress the differences between our Spanish and theirs, and thereby to disintegrate the language. I recall that when somebody or other scolded Roberto Arlt because he knew so little about Lunfardo, the putative language of the Buenos Aires underworld, he answered his critic in this way: "I was raised in Villa Luro, among thugs and bullies and poor people, and I really had very little time to study the way they talked." Lunfardo is, in fact, a literary put-on, a language invented by composers of tangos and writers of comedies for the stage and screen; the lowlifes and thugs themselves, those who lived in the tough, ragged outskirts of the city and who are supposed to have created it and used it in their daily lives, actually know nothing about it, except what phonograph records may have taught them.

I have set my stories at some distance in both time and space. Imagination has more freedom to work, that way. Today, in 1970, who can recall exactly what those outskirts of Palermo or Lomas were like at the end of the nineteenth century? Incredible as it may seem, there are certain punctilious men and women who act as a sort of "trivia police." They will note, for example, that Martín Fierro would have talked about a *bag* of bones, not a *sack*, and they will criticize (perhaps unfairly, perhaps not) the golden-pink coat of a certain horse famous in our literature.*

God save you, reader, from long forewords.—The quotation is from Quevedo, who (not to commit an anachronism that would have been caught sooner or later) never read the prefaces of Shaw.

J.L.B.

Buenos Aires, April 19, 1970

The Interloper

2 Reyes 1:26*

They say (though it seems unlikely) that Eduardo, the younger of the Nelson brothers, told the story in eighteen-ninety-something at the wake for Cristián, the elder, who had died of natural causes in the district of Morón. What is unquestionably true is that as the cups of *mate* went their rounds in the course of that long night when there was nothing else to do, somebody heard it from *someone* and later repeated it to Santiago Dabove, from whom I first heard it. I was told the story again, years later, in Turdera, where it had actually occurred. This second, somewhat less succinct version corroborated the essential details of Santiago's, with the small divergences and variations one always expects. I commit it to writing now because I believe it affords us (though I may of course be mistaken) a brief and tragic window on the sort of men that once fought their knife fights and lived their harsh lives in the tough neighborhoods on the outskirts of Buenos Aires. I will tell the story conscientiously, though I can foresee myself yielding to the literary temptation to heighten or insert the occasional small detail.

In Turdera they were known as the Nilsens. I was told by the parish priest that his predecessor recalled having seen, not without some surprise, a worn black-letter Bible in the house; on its last pages he had glimpsed handwritten names and dates. That black-bound volume was the only book they owned—its troubled chronicle of the Nilsens is now lost, as everything will one day be lost. The big ramshackle house (which is no longer standing) was of unplastered brick; from the entryway one could see a first interior patio of red tiles and another, farther back, of packed earth. Few people, however, entered that entryway; the Nilsens defended their solitude. They slept on cots in dilapidated and unfurnished bedrooms; their luxuries were horses, saddles, short-bladed daggers, flashy Saturday night clothes, and the alcohol that made them belligerent. I know that they were tall, with reddish hair—the blood of Denmark or Ireland (countries whose names they probably never heard) flowed in the veins of those two criollos.* The neighborhood was afraid of the Redheads, as they were called; it is not impossible that one or another killing had been their work. Once they had stood shoulder to shoulder and fought it out with the police. People say the younger brother had once traded words with Juan Iberra and not gone away with the worst of it—which according to those who knew about such things was saying a great deal. They were cattle drivers, teamsters, horse thieves, and sometime cardsharps. They had a reputation for tightfistedness, except when drinking and gambling made them generous. About their kinspeople, nothing is known even of where they came from. They owned an oxcart and a yoke of oxen.

Physically, they were unlike the toughs that gave Costa Brava* its reputation for lawlessness. That, and things we have no certain knowledge of, may help us understand how close they were. Having a falling-out with one of them was earning yourself two enemies.

The Nilsens were men who sought the pleasures of the flesh, but their romantic episodes had so far been on porches or in entryways or houses of ill repute. There was a good deal of talk, therefore, when Cristián carried Juliana Burgos home to live with him. The truth was, in doing so he had gained a servant, but it was also true that he lavished ghastly trinkets upon her and showed her off at parties—those shabby little tenement house parties where certain tango steps (the *quebrada* and the *corte*, for example) were considered indecent and weren't allowed, and where couples still danced "with a good bit of daylight between them," as the saying went. Juliana had almond eyes and dark skin; whenever someone looked at her she smiled. In a humble neighborhood, where work and neglect make women old before their time, she was not bad-looking.

At first, Eduardo lived with them. Then he went off to Arrecifes on some business, and on his return he brought a girl home with him, too; he had picked her up on the road. Within a few days he threw her out. He grew ever more sullen and bad-tempered; he would get drunk by himself in the corner general-store-and-bar and would not answer when someone spoke to him. He was in love with Cristián's woman. The neighborhood (which probably knew that before he himself did) sensed with secret and perfidious delight the latent rivalry that throbbed between the brothers.

One night, coming home late from a bout of drinking, Eduardo saw Cristián's black horse tied to the post at the front of the house. Cristián was sitting waiting for him in the patio; he was wearing his best clothes. The woman was walking about the house with her *mate* in her hand.

"I'm going off to that bust over at Farías' place. There's Juliana—if you want her, use her."

His tone was half-peremptory, half-cordial. Eduardo stood for a moment looking at him; he didn't know what to do. Cristián stood up, said good-bye to Eduardo—not to Juliana, who was a mere thing—mounted his horse, and rode off at an unhurried trot.

From that night onward, they shared her. No one will ever know the details of that sordid ménage, which outraged the neighborhood's sense of decency. The arrangement went well for a few weeks, but it couldn't last. Never, when the three of them were in the house, did the brothers speak Juliana's name, even to call her, but they looked for—and found—reasons to disagree. They bickered over the sale price of a load of skins, but it was something else they were really arguing about. Cristián's tendency was to raise his voice; Eduardo's, to fall silent. Without knowing it, they were jealous of each other. In those hard-bitten outskirts of the city, a man didn't say, nor was it said about him, that a woman mattered to him (beyond desire and ownership), but the two brothers were in fact in love. They felt humiliated by that, somehow.

One afternoon in the Lomas town plaza, Eduardo ran into Juan Iberra, who congratulated him on that beauty he'd found himself. It was then, I think, that Eduardo gave him a tongue-lashing. Nobody, in Eduardo's presence, was going to make Cristián the butt of such jokes.

The woman saw to the needs of both brothers with beastlike submissiveness, although she couldn't hide some preference for the younger, who had not refused to take part in the arrangement but hadn't initiated it, either.

One day, the brothers ordered Juliana to take two chairs out into the first patio and then make herself scarce; the two of them needed to talk. She was expecting a long talk, so she lay down for her siesta, but soon they called her back. They had her put everything she owned, even the rosary of glass beads and the little crucifix her mother had left her, in a sack. Without a word of explanation, they loaded her onto the oxcart and set off on a tedious and silent journey. It had rained; the roads were heavy, and it was sometime around five in the morning when they finally reached Morón. There, they woke up the madam of a whorehouse and offered to sell her Juliana. The deal was struck; Cristián took the money, and divided it later with Eduardo.

Back in Turdera, the Nilsens, who had been entangled in the thicket (which was also the routine) of that monstrous love, tried to take up their old life as men among men. They returned to their games of *truco*, their cockfights, their casual binges. They thought, once in a while, perhaps, that they were saved, but then, separately, they began to take unexplained (or overexplained) absences. Shortly before the end of the year, Eduardo announced that he had business in the capital, and he rode away. When he had gone, Cristián took the road to Morón; there, tied to the hitching post of the house which the story would lead us to expect, was Eduardo's pinto. Cristián went in; Eduardo was inside, waiting his turn.

Cristián, it seems, said to him. "If we keep on this way much longer, we're going to wear out the horses. Maybe we ought to have her where we can get at her."

He spoke to the madam, pulled some coins out of his purse, and they took Juliana away with them. She rode with Cristián; Eduardo put spurs to his palomino so he wouldn't have to see them.

They went back to the old arrangement. Their abominable solution had failed; both of them had given in to the temptation to cheat. Cain lurked about, but the love between the Nilsens was great (who can say what hardships and dangers they had shared!) and they chose to take their exasperation out on others: a stranger—the dogs—Juliana, who had introduced the seed of discord.

The month of March was nearing its close but the heat dragged on relentlessly. One Sunday (on Sunday people tended to call it a day early), Eduardo, who was coming home from the bar, saw that Cristián was yoking up the oxen.

"Come on," Cristián said, "we've got to take some skins over to the Nigger's place. I've already loaded them up—we can go in the cool of the evening."

The Nigger's store lay a little south of the Nilsens' place, I believe: they took the Troop Road, then turned off onto a road that was not so heavily traveled. The countryside grew larger and larger as the night came on.

They were driving along beside a field covered in dried-out

straw; Cristián threw out the cigar he had lighted and stopped the oxcart.

"Let's go to work, brother. The buzzards'll come in to clean up after us. I killed 'er today. We'll leave 'er here, her and her fancy clothes. She won't cause any more hurt."

Almost weeping, they embraced. Now they were linked by yet another bond: the woman grievously sacrificed, and the obligation to forget her.

Unworthy

The picture of the city that we carry in our mind is always slightly out of date. The café has degenerated into a bar; the vestibule that allowed us a glimpse of patio and grapevine is now a blurred hallway with an elevator down at the far end. Thus, for years I thought that a certain bookstore, the Librería Buenos Aires, would be awaiting me at a certain point along Calle Talcahuano, but then one morning I discovered that an antiques shop had taken the bookstore's place, and I was told that don Santiago Fischbein, the owner of the bookstore, had died. Fischbein had tended toward the obese; his features are not as clear in my memory as our long conversations are. Firmly yet coolly he would condemn Zionism—it would make the Jew an ordinary man, he said, tied like all other men to a single tradition and a single country, and bereft of the complexities and discords that now enrich him. I recall that he once told me that a new edition of the works of Baruch Spinoza was being prepared, which would banish all that Euclidean apparatus that makes Spinoza's work so difficult to read yet at the same time imparts an illusory sense of rigor to the fantastic theory. Fischbein showed me (though he refused to sell me) a curious copy of Rosenroth's *Kabbala Denudata*, but my library does contain some books by Ginsburg and Waite that bear Fischbein's seal.

One afternoon when the two of us were alone, he confided to me an episode of his life, and today I can tell it. I will change the occasional detail—as is only to be expected.

*

29

I am going to tell you about something (Fischbein began) that I have never told anyone before. My wife Ana doesn't know about this, nor do my closest friends. It happened so many years ago that it no longer feels like my own experience. Maybe you can use it for a story—no doubt you'll endow it with a knife fight or two. I don't know whether I've ever mentioned that I'm from Entre Ríos. I won't tell you that we were Jewish gauchos—there were never any Jewish gauchos. We were merchants and small farmers. I was born in Urdinarrain, which I only barely remember; when my parents came to Buenos Aires, to open a shop, I was just a little boy. The Maldonado* was a few blocks from us, and then came the empty lots.

Carlyle wrote that men need heroes. Grosso's *History* suggested that San Martín might be a fit object of worship, but all I ever saw in San Martín was a soldier who'd waged war in Chile and who'd now become a bronze statue and given his name to a plaza. Chance dealt me a very different hero, to the misfortune of us both: Francisco Ferrari. This is probably the first time you've ever heard of him.

Our neighborhood was not a bad one, the way Los Corrales and El Bajo were said to be, but every corner grocery-store-and-bar had its gang of toughs. Ferrari hung out in the one at Triunvirato and Thames. That was where the incident happened that led me to be one of his followers. I'd gone in to buy some yerba for the *mate*. A stranger with long hair and a mustache came in and ordered a gin.

"Say"—Ferrari's voice was as smooth as silk—"didn't I see you last night at the dance at Juliana's? Where're you from?"

"San Cristóbal," the other man replied.

"Well, I'll tell you for your own good," Ferrari said to him, "you ought to stay up there. There are people in this neighborhood that are liable to give you a hard time."

The man from San Cristóbal left, mustache and all. He may

have been no less a man than Ferrari, but he knew he was up against the whole gang.

From that afternoon on, Francisco Ferrari was the hero that my fifteen-year-old heart yearned for. He had black hair and was rather tall, good-looking—handsome in the style of those days. He always wore black. It was a second episode that actually brought us together. I was walking along with my mother and my aunt when we came upon some street toughs, and one of them said loudly to the others:

"Let the old hens through. Meat's too gristly to eat."

I didn't know what to do. But Ferrari, who was just coming out of his house, stepped in. He stood face to face with one who'd spoken, and he said:

"If you boys feel like picking a fight with somebody, why don't you pick a fight with me?"

He walked down the line, slowly, one by one, but nobody said a word. They knew him. He shrugged his shoulders, waved at us, and walked away. But before he left, he said to me:

"If you're not doing anything later on, stop by the joint."

I stood there unnerved and shaken. Sarah, my aunt, issued her verdict: "A gentleman that demands respect for ladies."

To save me from the spot that put me in, my mother corrected her:

"I would say, rather, a ruffian who won't allow competition."

I don't know how to explain it to you. Today I've carved out a place for myself. I have this bookstore that I enjoy and whose books I read; I have friendships, like ours; I have my wife and children; I've joined the Socialist Party—I'm a good Argentine and a good Jew. I am respected and respectable. The man you see now is almost bald; at that time I was a poor Jewish kid with red hair in a tough neighborhood on the outskirts of the city. People looked askance at me. I tried, as all young fellows do, to be like everyone else. I had started calling myself Santiago* to make the

Jacob go away, but there was nothing I could do about the Fischbein. We all come to resemble the image others have of us; I sensed people's contempt for me, and I felt contempt for myself as well. At that time, and especially in that setting, it was important to be brave; I knew myself to be a coward. Women intimidated me; deep down, I was ashamed of my fainthearted chastity. I had no friends my own age.

I didn't go to the corner bar that night. I wish I'd never gone. But little by little I became convinced that the invitation was an order. One Saturday after dinner, I went in.

Ferrari was presiding over one of the tables. I knew the others' faces; there were probably seven, all told. Ferrari was the oldest one there, except for one old man of few words, and weary ones, whose name is the only one that from my memory has not faded: don Eliseo Amaro. A knife scar crossed his face, which was very broad and slack. I learned sometime later that he'd once been in prison for something. . . .

Ferrari had me sit at his left; don Eliseo had to change seats. I was nervous. I was afraid Ferrari would make some allusion to the unfortunate incident of a few days before, you see. But nothing of the sort happened; they talked about women, cards, elections, an itinerant singer that was supposed to come but never did— the things going on in the neighborhood. At first it was hard for them to swallow the little red-haired Jewish kid; they finally did, though, because Ferrari wanted it that way. In spite of their names, which were mostly Italian, they all felt themselves (and were felt to be) native Argentines, even gauchos. Some were teamsters or cart drivers, and there may even have been a butcher; their work with animals gave them a bond with the countrypeople. I suspect that they wished more than anything that they had been born Juan Moreira.* They wound up calling me Little Sheeny,* but there was no contempt in the nickname. I learned from those men how to smoke, and other things.

One night in one of the houses on Calle Junín,* someone asked

me if I wasn't a friend of Francisco Ferrari's. I shook my head—
I felt I would be almost bragging if I said yes.

The police came into the bar one night and frisked everyone.
Several of us were taken to the police station—but they didn't
mess with Ferrari. Two weeks later the scene was repeated; this
second time, they arrested Ferrari too. He had a dagger in his
belt. He may have fallen out of favor with the ward boss.

Today I see Ferrari as a poor kid misguided and betrayed; at
the time, in my eyes, a god he was.

Friendship, you know, is as mysterious as love or any other
state of this confusion we call life. In fact, I have sometimes
suspected that the only thing that holds no mystery is happiness,
because it is its own justification. However that may be, the fact
was that Francisco Ferrari, the daring, strong Ferrari, felt a sense
of friendship for me, contemptible me. I felt he was mistaken, that
I was not worthy of that friendship. I tried to avoid him, but he
wouldn't let me. My anxiety was made worse by my mother's
disapproval; she could not resign herself to my associating with
what she called "the riffraff," nor to the fact that I'd begun to ape
them. The essential element in the story I am telling you, though,
is my relationship with Ferrari, not the sordid events themselves,
which I do not now regret. "So long as regret lasts, guilt lasts."

One night I came into the bar to find the old man, don Eliseo,
who had taken his place again beside Ferrari, in whispered
conversation with him. They were plotting something. From the
other end of the table, I thought I heard the name Weidemann—
Weidemann's weaving mill stood on the outskirts of the neighborhood. In a few minutes Ferrari and don Eliseo sent me off to have
a look around the factory. I was given no explanation, but I was
told to pay special attention to the doors. Night was falling when
I crossed the Maldonado and the railroad tracks. I recall a few
scattered houses, a stand of willow trees, and vacant lots. The
factory was new, but it had a solitary, seedy look about it; in my
memory now, its reddish color mingles with the sunset. There

not "it was," but instead
"i remember it as"

33

was a fence around it. Besides the main door, there were two doors in back, facing south, that opened directly into the workshops.

I confess it took me some time to grasp what I imagine you've already grasped. I made my report, which one of the other kids corroborated—his sister worked in the factory. If the gang had missed a Saturday night at the bar, everyone would have remembered, so Ferrari decided the robbery would take place the next Friday. I was to be the lookout. Meanwhile, it was best that no one see us together.

When we were alone together in the street outside, I asked Ferrari whether he really trusted me with this mission.

unexpected

"Yes," he said. "I know you'll comport yourself like a man."

→ I slept well that night, and the nights that followed as well. On Wednesday I told my mother I was going downtown to see a new cowboy movie. I put on the best clothes I owned and set off for Calle Moreno. The trip on the streetcar was a long one. At the police station they made me wait, but finally one of the clerks, a man named Eald or Alt, would see me. I told him I had come to discuss a confidential matter. He told me I could speak freely. I told him what Ferrari was planning to do. I was astounded that the name was unknown to him; it was another thing when I mentioned don Eliseo.

"Ah!" he said, "he was one of the Uruguayan's gang."

Eald or Alt sent for another officer, one assigned to my precinct, and the two of them consulted. One of them asked me, not with sarcasm:

"Are you making this accusation because you think you're a good citizen? Is that it?"

I didn't feel he'd understand, so I answered.

"Yes, sir. I am a good Argentine."

They told me to carry out the orders the leader of my gang had given me, all except the part about whistling when I saw the police coming. As I was leaving, one of them warned me:

"Be careful. You know what happens to squealers."

Police officers love to show off their Lunfardo,* like fourth graders.

"I hope they kill me," I answered. "It's the best thing that could happen to me."

Beginning early Friday morning and all throughout that day, I was filled with a sense of relief that the day had come at last, and of remorse at feeling no remorse whatever. The hours seemed endless. I barely touched my food. At ten that night we began gathering, less than a block from the factory. There was one of us that didn't come; don Eliseo said there was always one washout. It occurred to me that the blame for what was to happen would fall on the absent man. It was about to rain. I was afraid that one of the others might stay behind with me, but I was left by myself at one of the back doors. Pretty soon the police came, an officer and several patrolmen. They came on foot, for stealth; they had left their horses in a field. Ferrari had forced the factory door, so the police were able to slip inside without a sound. Then I was stunned to hear four shots. There inside, in the darkness, I thought, they were killing each other. Then I saw the police come out with the men in handcuffs. Then two more policemen emerged, dragging the bodies of Francisco Ferrari and don Eliseo Amaro, who'd been shot at point-blank range. In their report the police said the robbers had failed to halt when they were ordered, and that Ferrari and don Eliseo had fired the first shots. I knew that was a lie, because I had never seen either of them with a revolver. The police had taken advantage of the occasion to settle an old score. Days later, I was told that Ferrari tried to get away, but one shot was all it took. The newspapers, of course, made him the hero that perhaps he never was, but that I had dreamed of.

I was arrested with the others, but a short while later they let me go.

The Story from Rosendo Juárez

It was about eleven o'clock one night; I had gone into the old-fashioned general-store-and-bar, which is now simply a bar, on the corner of Bolívar and Venezuela.* As I went in, I noticed that over in a corner, sitting at one of the little tables, was a man I had never seen before. He hissed to catch my eye and motioned me to come over. He must have looked like a man that one didn't want to cross, because I went at once toward his table. I felt, inexplicably, that he had been sitting there for some time, in that chair, before that empty glass. He was neither tall nor short; he looked like an honest craftsman, or perhaps an old-fashioned country fellow. His sparse mustache was grizzled. A bit stiff, as Porteños tend to be, he had not taken off his neck scarf.* He offered to buy me a drink; I sat down and we chatted. All this happened in nineteen-thirty-something.

"You've heard of me, sir, though we've never met," the man began, "but I know you. My name is Rosendo Juárez. It was Nicolás Paredes, no doubt, God rest his soul, that told you about me. That old man was something. I'll tell you—the stories he'd tell. . . .Not so as to fool anyone, of course—just to be entertaining. But since you and I are here with nothing else on our hands just now, I'd like to tell you what really happened that night . . . the night the Yardmaster was murdered. You've put the story in a novel,* sir—and I'm hardly qualified to judge that novel—but I want you to know the truth behind the lies you wrote."

He paused, as though to put his recollections in order, and then he began. . . .

Things happen to a man, you see, and a man only understands them as the years go by. What happened to me that night had been waiting to happen for a long time. I was brought up in the neighborhood of the Maldonado,* out beyond Floresta. It was one big open sewage ditch back then, if you know what I mean, but fortunately they've run sewer lines in there now. I've always been of the opinion that nobody has the right to stand in the way of progress. You just do the best you can with the hand you're dealt. . . .

It never occurred to me to find out the name of the father that begot me. Clementina Juárez, my mother, was a good honest woman that earned her living with her iron. If you were to ask me, I'd say she was from Entre Ríos or the Banda Oriental, what people now call Uruguay; be that as it may, she would always talk about her relatives over in Uruguay, in Concepción. For myself, I grew up the best I could. I learned to knife fight with the other boys, using a charred piece of stick. That was before we were all taken over by soccer, which back at that time was still just something the English did.

Anyway, while I was sitting in the bar one night, this fellow named Garmendia started trying to pick a fight with me. I ignored him for a while—playing deaf, you might say—but this Garmendia, who was feeling his liquor, kept egging me on. We finally took it outside; out on the sidewalk, Garmendia turned back a second, pushed the door open again a little, and announced— "Not to worry, boys, I'll be right back."

I had borrowed a knife. We walked down toward the Maldonado, slow, watching each other. He was a few years older than I was; he and I had practiced knife fighting together lots of times, and I had a feeling I was going to get positively gutted. I

37

was walking down the right-hand side of the alley, and him down the left. Suddenly, he tripped over some big chunks of cement that were lying there. The second he tripped, I jumped him, almost without thinking about it. I cut his cheek open with one slash, then we locked together—there was a second when anything could've happened—and then I stabbed him once, which was all it took. . . .It was only sometime later that I realized he'd left his mark on me, too—scratches, though, that was about it. I learned that night that it isn't hard to kill a man, or get killed yourself. The creek was down; to keep the body from being found too soon, I half-hid it behind a brick kiln. I was so stunned I suppose I just stopped thinking, because I slipped off the ring Garmendia always wore and put it on. Then I straightened my hat and went back to the bar. I walked in as easy as you please.

"Looks like it's me that's come back," I said.

I ordered a shot of brandy, and the truth is, I needed it. That was when somebody pointed out the bloodstain.

That night I tossed and turned on my bunk all night; I didn't fall asleep till nearly dawn. About the time of early mass, two cops came looking for me. You should have seen the way my mother carried on, may she rest in peace, poor thing. I was dragged off like a criminal. Two days and two nights I sat in that stinking cell. Nobody came to visit me—except for Luis Irala, a true friend if ever there was one. But they wouldn't let him see me. Then one morning the captain sent for me. He was sitting there in his chair; he didn't even look at me at first, but he did speak.

"So you put Garmendia out of his misery?" he said.

"If you say so," I answered.

"It's 'sir' to you. And we'll have no ducking or dodging, now. Here are the statements from the witnesses, and here's the ring that was found in your house. Just sign the confession and get this over with."

He dipped the pen in the inkwell and handed it to me.

"Let me think about this, captain.—Sir," I added.

"I'll give you twenty-four hours to think about it real good, in your very own cell. I won't rush you. But if you decide not to see things in a reasonable way, you'd best start getting used to the idea of a vacation down on Calle Las Heras."

As you might imagine, I didn't understand that right away.

"If you decide to come around, you'll just be in for a few days. I'll let you go—don Nicolás Paredes has promised me he'll fix it for you."

But it was *ten* days. I'd almost given up hope when they finally remembered me. I signed what they put in front of me to sign and one of the cops took me over to Calle Cabrera. . . .*

There were horses tied to the hitching post, and standing out on the porch and all inside the place there were more people than a Saturday night at the whorehouse. It looked like a party committee headquarters. Don Nicolás, who was sipping at a *mate*, finally called me over. As calm as you please, he told me he was going to send me out to Morón, where they were setting up for the elections. He told me to look up a certain Sr. Laferrer; he'd try me out, he said. The letter I was to take was written by a kid in black that wrote poems* about tenement houses and riffraff— or anyway, that's what I was told. I can't imagine that educated people would be much interested in that sort of thing, much less if it's told in poetry. Anyway, I thanked Paredes for the favor, and I left. The cop didn't stay so infernally glued to me on the way back.

So it all turned out for the best. Providence knows what it's doing. Garmendia's killing, which at first had got me in such hot water, was now starting to open doors for me. Of course the cops had me over a barrel—if I didn't work out, if I didn't toe the line for the party, I'd be hauled in again. But I'd got some heart back, and I had faith in myself.

Laferrer warned me right off that I was going to have to walk the straight and narrow with him, but if I did, he said, he might make me his bodyguard. The work I did for 'em was all anyone could ask. In Morón, and later on in the neighborhood too, I gradually won my bosses' trust. The police and the party gradually spread the word that I was a man to be reckoned with; I was an important cog in the wheels of the elections in Buenos Aires, and out in the province too. Elections were fierce back then; I won't bore you, señor, with stories about the blood that would be shed. I did all I could to make life hard on the radicals, though to this day they're still riding on Alem's coattails. But as I say, there was no man that didn't show me respect. I got myself a woman, La Lujanera we called her, and a handsome copper sorrel. For years I pretended to be some kind of Moreira*—who in his day was probably imitating some other stage show gaucho. I played a lot of cards and drank a lot of absinthe. . . .

We old folks talk and talk and talk, I know, but I'm coming to what I wanted to tell you. I don't know if I mentioned Luis Irala. A true friend, the likes of which you'll not often find. . . .He was getting on in years when I knew him, and he'd never been afraid of hard work; for some reason he took a liking to me. He'd never set foot in a committee room—he earned his living carpentering. He didn't stick his nose in anybody else's business, and he didn't let anybody stick their nose in his. One morning he came to see me.

"I guess you've heard Casilda left me," he said. "Rufino Aguilera is the man that took her away from me."

I'd had dealings with that particular individual in Morón.

"I know Rufino," I told him. "I'd have to say that of all the Aguileras, he's the least disgusting."

"Disgusting or not, I've got a bone to pick with him."

I thought for a minute.

"Listen," I finally told him, "nobody takes anything away from anybody. If Casilda left you, it's because it's Rufino she wants, and she's not interested in you."

"But what'll people say? That I'm yellow? That I don't stand up to a man that wrongs me?"

"My advice to you is not to go looking for trouble because of what people might say, let alone because of a woman that doesn't love you anymore."

"I couldn't care less about her," he said. "A man that thinks longer than five minutes running about a woman is no man, he's a pansy. And Casilda's heartless, anyway. The last night we spent together she told me I was getting old."

"She was telling you the truth."

"And it hurts, but it's beside the point—Rufino's the one I'm after now."

"You want to be careful there," I told him. "I've seen Rufino in action, in the Merlo elections. He's like greased lightning."

"You think I'm afraid of Rufino Aguilera?"

"I know you're not afraid of him, but think about it—one of two things will happen: either you kill him and you get sent off to stir, or he kills you and you get sent off to Chacarita."*

"One of two things. So tell me, what would you do in my place?"

"I don't know, but then I'm not exactly the best example to follow. I'm a guy that to get his backside out of jail has turned into a gorilla for the party."

"I'm not planning to turn into a gorilla for the party, I'm planning to collect a debt a man owes me."

"You mean you're going to stake your peace of mind on a stranger you've never met and a woman you don't even love anymore?"

But Luis Irala wasn't interested in hearing what I had to say, so he left. The next day we heard that he'd picked a fight with Rufino in some bar over in Morón and that Rufino had killed him.

He went off to get killed, and he got himself killed right honorably, too—man to man. I'd done the best I could, I'd given him a friend's advice, but I still felt guilty.

A few days after the wake, I went to the cockfights. I'd never been all that keen on cockfights, but that Sunday, I'll tell you the truth, they made me sick. What in the world's wrong with those animals, I thought, that they tear each other to pieces this way, for no good reason?

The night of this story I'm telling you, the night of the end of the story, the boys and I had all gone to a dance over at the place that a black woman we called La Parda ran. Funny—all these years, and I still remember the flowered dress La Lujanera was wearing that night. . . .The party was out in the patio. There was the usual drunk trying to pick a fight, but I made sure things went the way they were supposed to go. It was early, couldn't have been midnight yet, when the strangers showed up. One of them—they called him the Yardmaster, and he was stabbed in the back and killed that very night, just the way you wrote it, sir—anyway, this one fellow bought a round of drinks for the house. By coincidence this Yardmaster and I were dead ringers for each other. He had something up his sleeve that night: he came up to me and started laying it on pretty thick—he was from up north, he said, and he'd been hearing about me. He couldn't say enough about my reputation. I let him talk, but I was beginning to suspect what was coming. He was hitting the gin hard, too, and I figured it was to get his courage up—and sure enough, pretty soon he challenged me to a fight. That was when it happened—what nobody wants to understand. I looked at that swaggering drunk just spoiling for a fight, and it was like I was looking at myself in a mirror, and all of a sudden I was ashamed of myself. I wasn't afraid of him; if I had been, I might've gone outside and fought him. I just stood there. This other guy, this Yardmaster, who by now had his face about this far from mine, raised his voice so everybody could hear him:

"You know what's wrong with you? You're yellow, that's what's wrong with you!"

"That may be," I said. "I can live with being called yellow. You can tell people you called me a son of a whore, too, and say

I let you spit in my face. Now then, does that make you feel better?"

La Lujanera slipped her hand up my sleeve and pulled out the knife I always carried there and slipped it into my hand. And to make sure I got the message, she also said, "Rosendo, I think you're needing this." Her eyes were blazing.

I dropped the knife and walked out—taking my time about it. People stepped back to make way for me. They couldn't believe their eyes. What did I care what they thought.

To get out of that life, I moved over to Uruguay and became an oxcart driver. Since I came back, I've made my place here. San Telmo* has always been a peaceful place to live.

The Encounter

For Susana Bombal

Those who read the news each morning do so simply to forget it again, or for the sake of the evening's conversation, and so it should surprise no one that people no longer remember, or remember as though in a dream, the once-famous and much-discussed case of Maneco Uriarte and a man named Duncan. Of course the event took place in 1910, the year of the comet and the Centennial, and we have had and lost so many things since then. . . . The protagonists are dead now; those who were witness to the event swore an oath of solemn silence. I too raised my hand to swear, and I felt, with all the romantic seriousness of my nine or ten years, the gravity of that rite. I can't say whether the others noticed that I gave my word; I can't say whether they kept their own. However that may be, this is the story—with the inevitable changes that time, and good (or bad) literature, occasion.

That evening, my cousin Lafinur had taken me to an *asado*, one of those gatherings of men with the roasting of the fatted calf (or lamb, as it turned out to be), at a country place called Los Laureles. I cannot describe the topography; we should picture a town in the north of the country—peaceful and shady, and sloping down gently toward the river—rather than some flat, sprawling city. The journey by train lasted long enough for me to find it boring, but childhood's time, as we all know, flows slowly. Dusk had begun to settle when we drove through the gate to the large country house. There, I sensed, were the ancient elemental things: the smell of the meat as it turned golden on the spit, the trees, the dogs, the dry branches, the fire that brings men together.

There were no more than a dozen guests, all adults. (The oldest, I discovered later, was not yet thirty.) They were learnèd, I soon realized, in subjects that to this day I am unworthy of: racehorses, tailoring, automobiles, notoriously expensive women. No one disturbed my shyness, no one paid any mind to me. The lamb, prepared with slow skillfulness by one of the peons that worked on the estate, held us long in the dining room. The dates of the wines were discussed. There was a guitar; my cousin, I think I recall, sang Elías Regules' *La tapera* and *El gaucho* and a few *décimas* in Lunfardo,* which was *de rigueur* back then—verses about a knife fight in one of those houses on Calle Junín.* Coffee was brought in, and cigars. Not a word about heading back home. I felt, as Lugones once put it, "the fear of the lateness of the hour." I couldn't bring myself to look at the clock. To hide the loneliness I felt at being a boy among men, I drank down, without much pleasure, a glass or two of wine. Suddenly, Uriarte loudly challenged Duncan to a game of poker, just the two of them, *mano a mano*. Someone objected that two-handed poker usually was a sorry sort of game, and suggested a table of four. Duncan was in favor of that, but Uriarte, with an obstinacy that I didn't understand (and didn't try to), insisted that it be just the two of them. Outside of *truco* (whose essential purpose is to fill time with verses and good-natured mischief) and the modest labyrinths of solitaire, I have never cared much for cards. I slipped out of the room without anyone's noticing.

A big house that one has never been in before, its rooms in darkness (there was light only in the dining room), means more to a boy than an unexplored country to a traveler. Step by step I explored the house; I recall a billiard room, a conservatory with glass panes of rectangles and lozenges, a pair of rocking chairs, and a window from which there was a glimpse of a gazebo. In the dimness, I became lost; the owner of the house—whose name, after all these years, might have been Acevedo or Acébal—finally found me. Out of kindness, or, being a collector, out of vanity, he led me to a sort of museum case. When he turned on the light, I saw that it contained knives of every shape and kind, knives made famous by the circumstances of their use. He told me he had a little place near Pergamino, and that he had gathered his collection over years of traveling back and forth through the province. He opened the case and without looking at the little show cards for each piece he recounted the knives' histories, which were always more or less the same, with differences of place and date. I asked if among his knives he had the dagger that had been carried by Moreira* (at that time the very archetype of the gaucho, as Martín Fierro and Don Segundo Sombra* would later be). He had to admit he didn't, but he said he could show me one like it, with the same U-shaped cross guard. Angry voices interrupted him. He closed the case immediately; I followed him.

Uriarte was shouting that Duncan had been cheating. The others were standing around them. Duncan, I recall, was taller than the others; he was a sturdy-looking, inexpressive man a bit heavy in the shoulders, and his hair was so blond that it was almost white. Maneco Uriarte was a man of many nervous gestures and quick movements; he was dark, with features that revealed, perhaps, some trace of Indian blood, and a sparse, petulant mustache. Clearly, they were all drunk; I cannot say for certain whether there were two or three bottles scattered about on the floor or whether the cinematographer's abuses have planted that false memory in my mind. Uriarte's cutting (and now obscene) insults never ceased. Duncan seemed not to hear him; finally he stood up, as though weary, and hit Uriarte, once, in the face. Uriarte screamed—from the floor where he now lay sprawling— that he was not going to tolerate such an affront, and he challenged Duncan to fight.

Duncan shook his head.

"To tell the truth, I'm afraid of you," he added, by way of explanation.

A general burst of laughter greeted this.

"You're going to fight me, and now," Uriarte replied, once more on his feet.

Someone, God forgive him, remarked that there was no lack of weapons.

I am not certain who opened the vitrine. Maneco Uriarte selected the longest and showiest knife, the one with the U-shaped cross guard; Duncan, almost as though any one of them would serve as well as any other, chose a wood-handled knife with the figure of a little tree on the blade. Someone said it was like Maneco to choose a sword. No one was surprised that Maneco's hand should be shaking at such a moment; everyone was surprised to see that Duncan's was.

Tradition demands that when men fight a duel, they not sully the house they are in, but go outside for their encounter. Half in sport, half serious, we went out into the humid night. I was not drunk from wine, but I was drunk from the adventure; I yearned for someone to be killed, so that I could tell about it later, and remember it. Perhaps just then the others were no more adult than I. I also felt that a whirlpool we seemed incapable of resisting was pulling us down, and that we were about to be lost. No one really took Maneco's accusation seriously; everyone interpreted it as stemming from some old rivalry, tonight exacerbated by the wine.

We walked through the woods that lay out beyond the gazebo. Uriarte and Duncan were ahead of us; I thought it odd that they should watch each other the way they did, as though each feared a surprise move by the other. We came to a grassy patch.

"This place looks all right," Duncan said with soft authority.

The two men stood in the center indecisively.

"Throw down that hardware—it just gets in the way. Wrestle each other down for real!" a voice shouted.

But by then the men were fighting. At first they fought clumsily, as though afraid of being wounded; at first they watched their opponent's blade, but then they watched his eyes. Uriarte had forgotten about his anger; Duncan, his indifference or disdain. Danger had transfigured them; it was now two men, not two boys, that were fighting. I had imagined a knife fight as a chaos of steel, but I was able to follow it, or almost follow it, as though it were a game of chess. Time, of course, has not failed both to exalt and to obscure what I saw. I am not sure how long it lasted; there are events that cannot be held to ordinary measures of time.

As their forearms (with no ponchos wrapped around them for protection) blocked the thrusts, their sleeves, soon cut to ribbons, grew darker and darker with their blood. It struck me that we'd been mistaken in assuming they were unfamiliar with the knife. I began to see that the two men handled their weapons differently. The weapons were unequal; to overcome that disadvantage, Duncan tried to stay close to the other man, while Uriarte drew away in order to make long, low thrusts.

"They're killing each other! Stop them!" cried the same voice that had mentioned the showcase.

No one summoned the courage to intervene. Uriarte had lost ground; Duncan then charged him. Their bodies were almost touching now. Uriarte's blade sought Duncan's face. Abruptly it looked shorter; it had plunged into his chest. Duncan lay on the grass. It was then that he spoke, his voice barely audible:

"How strange. All this is like a dream."

He did not close his eyes, he did not move, and I had seen one man kill another.

Maneco Uriarte leaned down to the dead man and begged him to forgive him. He was undisguisedly sobbing. The act he had just committed overwhelmed and terrified him. I now know that he regretted less having committed a crime than having committed an act of senselessness.

I couldn't watch anymore. What I had longed to see happen had happened, and I was devastated. Lafinur later told me that they had to wrestle with the body to pull the knife out. A council was held among them, and they decided to lie as little as possible; the knife fight would be elevated to a duel with swords. Four of the men would claim to have been the seconds, among them Acébal. Everything would be taken care of in Buenos Aires; somebody always has a friend. . . .

On the mahogany table lay a confusion of playing cards and bills that no one could bring himself to look at or touch.

In the years that followed, I thought more than once about confiding the story to a friend, but I always suspected that I derived more pleasure from keeping the secret than I would from telling it. In 1929, a casual conversation suddenly moved me to break the long silence. José Olave, the retired chief of police, had been telling me stories of the knife fighters that hung out in the tough neighborhoods of Retiro, down near the docks—El Bajo and that area. He said men such as that were capable of anything—ambush, betrayal, trickery, the lowest and most infamous kind of villainy—in order to get the better of their opponents, and he remarked that before the Podestás and the Gutiérrezes,* there'd been very little knife fighting, the hand-to-hand sort of thing. I told him that I'd once actually witnessed such a fight, and then I told the story of that night so many years before.

He listened to me with professional attention, and then he asked me a question:

"Are you sure Uriarte and the other man had never used a knife in a fight before? That a stretch in the country at one time or another hadn't taught them something?"

"No," I replied. "Everyone there that night knew everyone else, and none of them could believe their eyes."

Olave went on unhurriedly, as though thinking out loud.

"You say one of those daggers had a U-shaped cross guard. . . .There were two famous daggers like that—the one that Moreira used and the one that belonged to Juan Almada, out around Tapalquén."

Something stirred in my memory.

"You also mentioned a wood-handled knife," Olave went on, "with the mark of a little tree on the blade. There are thousands of knives like that; that was the mark of the company that made them. But there was one . . ."

He stopped a moment, then went on:

"There was an Acevedo that had a country place near Pergamino. And there was another brawler of some repute that made his headquarters in that area at the turn of the century—Juan Almanza. From the first man he killed, at the age of fourteen, he always used one of those short knives, because he said it brought him luck. There was bad blood between Juan Almanza and Juan Almada, because people got them mixed up—their names, you see. . . .They kept their eyes open for each other a long time, but somehow their paths never crossed. Juan Almanza was killed by a stray bullet in some election or other. The other one, I think, finally died of old age in the hospital at Las Flores."

Nothing more was said that afternoon; we both sat thinking.

Nine or ten men, all of them now dead, saw what my eyes saw—the long thrust at the body and the body sprawled beneath the sky—but what they saw was the end of another, older story. Maneco Uriarte did not kill Duncan; it was the weapons, not the men, that fought. They had lain sleeping, side by side, in a cabinet, until hands awoke them. Perhaps they stirred when they awoke; perhaps that was why Uriarte's hand shook, and Duncan's as well. The two knew how to fight—the knives, I mean, not the men, who were merely their instruments—and they fought well that night. They had sought each other for a long time, down the long roads of the province, and at last they had found each other; by that time their gauchos were dust. In the blades of those knives there slept, and lurked, a human grudge.

Things last longer than men. Who can say whether the story ends here; who can say that they will never meet again.

Juan Muraña

For years I said I was brought up in Palermo.* It was, I know now, mere literary braggadocio, because the fact is, I grew up within the precincts of a long fence made of spear-tipped iron lances, in a house with a garden and my father's and grandfather's library. The Palermo of knife fights and guitars was to be found (I have been given to understand) on the street corners and in the bars and tenement houses.

In 1930, I devoted an essay to Evaristo Carriego, our neighbor, a poet whose songs glorified those neighborhoods on the outskirts of the city. A short time after that, chance threw Emilio Trápani in my way. I was taking the train to Morón; Trápani, who was sitting beside the window, spoke to me by name. It took me a moment to recognize him; so many years had gone by since we shared a bench in that school on Calle Thames. (Roberto Godel will recall that.) Trápani and I had never particularly liked each other; time, and reciprocal indifference, had put even greater distance between us. It was he, I now remember, who had taught me the rudiments of Lunfardo—the thieves' jargon of the day. There on the train we fell into one of those trivial conversations that are bent upon dredging up pointless information and that sooner or later yield the news of the death of a schoolmate who's nothing but a name to us anymore. Then suddenly Trápani changed the subject.

"Somebody lent me your book on Carriego," he said. "It's full of knife fighters and thugs and underworld types. Tell me,

51

Borges," he said, looking at me as though stricken with holy terror, "what can *you* know about knife fighters and thugs and underworld types?"

"I've read up on the subject," I replied.

"'Read up on it' is right," he said, not letting me go on. "But I don't need to 'read up'—I know those people."

After a silence, he added, as though sharing a secret with me: "I am a nephew of Juan Muraña."*

Of all the knife fighters in Palermo in the nineties, Muraña was the one that people talked about most.

"Florentina, my mother's sister," he went on, "was Muraña's wife. You might be interested in the story."

Certain rhetorical flourishes and one or another overlong sentence in Trápani's narration made me suspect that this was not the first time he had told it.

It was always a source of chagrin to my mother that her sister would marry Juan Muraña, whom my mother considered a cold-blooded rogue, though Florentina saw him as a "man of action." There were many versions of the fate that befell my uncle. There were those who claimed that one night when he'd been drinking he fell off the seat of his wagon as he turned the corner of Coronel and cracked his skull on the cobblestones. Some said the law was after him and he ran off to Uruguay. My mother, who could never bear her brother-in-law, never explained it to me. I was just a tyke, and I don't really even remember him.

Around the time of the Centennial,* we were living on Russell Alley. It was a long, narrow house we lived in, so while the front door was on Russell, the back door, which was always locked, was on San Salvador. My aunt, who was getting on in years and had become a little odd, lived in a bedroom in the attic. A skinny, bony woman she was, or so she seemed to me—tall, and miserly with her words. She was afraid of fresh air, never went outside, and she wouldn't let us come in her room; more than once I caught her stealing food and hiding it. Around the neighborhood, people would sometimes say that Muraña's death, or disappearance, had driven her insane. I always picture her dressed in black. She'd taken to talking to herself.

The owner of our house was a man named Luchessi* who had a barbershop in Barracas.* My mother, who worked at home as a seamstress, was having a hard time making ends meet. Though I didn't really understand it all, I would overhear certain whispered words: *justice of the peace, dispossession, eviction for nonpayment.* My mother suffered terribly; my aunt would stubbornly say that Juan would never let that wop* throw us out. She would recall the case—which she'd told us about dozens of times—of a scurrilous thug from the Southside who'd had the audacity to cast aspersions on her husband's courage. When Juan Muraña found out, he'd gone all the way to the other side of the city, found the man, settled the dispute with one thrust of his knife, and thrown the body in the Riachuelo. I can't say whether the story was true; the important thing at the time was that it had been told and believed.

I pictured myself sleeping in the archways on Calle Serrano, or begging, or standing on a corner with a basket of peaches. I half liked the idea of selling peaches—it would get me out of going to school.

I'm not certain how long all the worrying and anguish lasted. Your father, rest his soul, told us once that time can't be measured in days the way money is measured in pesos and centavos, because all pesos are equal, while every day, perhaps every hour, is different. I didn't fully understand what he meant then, but the phrase stayed in my mind.

One night during this time, I had a dream that turned into a nightmare. It was a dream about my uncle Juan. I'd never known him, but in my dream he was a strong, muscular man with Indian features and a sparse mustache and long flowing hair. We were riding toward the south, through big quarries and stands of underbrush, but those quarries and stands of underbrush were also Calle Thames.* In my dream, the sun was high in the sky. Uncle Juan was dressed all in black. He stopped in a narrow pass, near some sort of scaffolding. He had his hand under his coat, over his heart—not like a man who's about to draw his weapon, but like one who's trying to hide it. He said to me, in a voice filled with sadness, "I've changed a great deal." Then he slowly pulled out his hand, and what I saw was a vulture's claw. I woke up screaming in the dark.

The next day my mother told me she was taking me with her to see Luchessi. I knew she was going to ask for more time; she was taking me along, I'm sure, so the landlord could see how pathetic she was. She didn't say a word to her sister, who would never have allowed her to lower herself that way. I'd never been in Barracas; to my eyes there were more people, more traffic, and fewer vacant lots than where we lived. When we came to a certain corner, we saw policemen and a crowd in front of the number we were looking for. One man who lived there on the street was going from group to group, telling the story of how he'd been awakened at three in the morning by banging noises; he'd heard the door open and somebody step inside. Nobody had ever closed the door—at dawn Luchessi was found lying in the entryway, half dressed. He'd been stabbed repeatedly. He had lived alone; the police never found the culprit. Nothing had been stolen. Someone recalled that recently the deceased man had been losing his eyesight. "His time had come," another person said in a voice of authority. That verdict, and the tone with which it was delivered, impressed me; as the years have gone by I've noticed that whenever someone dies, there's always some sententious soul who has the same revelation.

At the wake, somebody brought around coffee and I drank a cup. There was a wax dummy in the coffin instead of the dead man. I mentioned this fact to my mother; one of the mourners laughed and assured me that the figure dressed in black was indeed Sr. Luchessi. I stood there fascinated, staring at him. My mother had to take me by the arm and pull me away.

For months people talked about nothing else. Crimes were rare then; think of how much talk there was about the Longhair and Squealer and Chairmaker affair. The only person in Buenos Aires utterly unconcerned by the scandal was my aunt Florentina. With the insistence of old age, all she would say when the subject was brought up was, "I told you people that Juan would never stand for that wop putting us out in the street."

One day there was a terrible storm; it seemed as though the sky had opened and the clouds had burst. Since I couldn't go to school, I started opening doors and drawers and cabinets, rummaging inside the way boys do, to see what secret treasures the house might hide. After a while I went up into the attic. There was my aunt, sitting with her hands folded in her lap; I sensed that she wasn't even thinking. Her room smelled musty. In one corner stood the iron bed, with a rosary hanging on one of the bedposts; in another, the wooden wardrobe for her clothes. On one of the whitewashed walls there was a lithograph of the Virgen del Carmen. A candlestick sat on the nightstand.

"I know what brings you up here," my aunt said, without raising her eyes. "Your mother sent you. She can't get it through her head that it was Juan that saved us."

"Juan?" I managed to say. "Juan died over ten years ago."

"Juan is here," she said. "You want to see him?"

She opened the drawer of the nightstand and took out a dagger.

"Here he is," she said softly. "I knew he'd never leave me. There's never been a man like him on earth. The wop never had a chance."

It was only then that I understood. That poor foolish, misdirected woman had murdered Luchessi. Driven by hatred, madness—perhaps, who knows, even love—she had slipped out the back door, made her way through one street after another in the night, and come at last to the house. Then, with those big bony hands, she had plunged the dagger into his chest. The dagger was Muraña, it was the dead man that she went on loving.

I'll never know whether she told my mother. She died a short time before we were evicted.

That was the end of the story that Trápani told me. I've never seen him again since. In the tale of that woman left all alone in the world, the woman who confuses her man, her tiger, with that cruel object he has bequeathed to her, the weapon of his bloody deeds, I believe one can make out a symbol, or many symbols. Juan Muraña was a man who walked my own familiar streets, who knew and did the things that men know and do, who one day tasted death, and who then became a knife. Now he is the memory of a knife. Tomorrow—oblivion, the common oblivion, forgotten.

The Elderly Lady

On January 14, 1941, María Justina Rubio de Jáuregui would celebrate her hundredth birthday. She was the only living child of the soldiers who had fought the wars of independence.*

Colonel Mariano Rubio, her father, was what might without irony or disrespect be called a minor national hero. Born the son of provincial landowners in the parish of La Merced, Rubio was promoted to second lieutenant in the Army of the Andes and served at Chacabuco, at the defeat at Cancha Rayada, at Maipú, and, two years later, at Arequipa.* The story is told that on the eve of that action, he and José de Olavarría exchanged swords.* In early April of '23 there took place the famous Battle of Cerro Alto, which, since it was fought in the valley, is also called the Battle of Cerro Bermejo.* Always envious of our Argentine glories, the Venezuelans have attributed that victory to General Simón Bolívar, but the impartial observer, the *Argentine* historian, is not so easily taken in; he knows very well that the laurels won there belong to Colonel Mariano Rubio. It was Rubio, at the head of a regiment of Colombian hussars, who turned the tide of the uncertain battle waged with saber and lance, the battle that in turn prepared the way for the no less famous action at Ayacucho,* in which Rubio also fought, and indeed was wounded. In '27 he acquitted himself with courage at Ituzaingó,* where he served under the immediate command of Carlos María Alvear.* In spite of his kinship with Rosas,* Rubio was a Lavalle man, a supporter of the Unitarian party, and he dispersed the *montonero* insurgents* in an action that he always characterized as "taking a swipe at them with our sabers."

When the Unitarians were defeated, Rubio left Argentina for Uruguay. There, he married. During the course of the Great War he died in Montevideo, which was under siege by Oribe's White* army. He was just short of his forty-fourth birthday, which at that time was virtually old age. He was a friend of Florencio Varela's. It is entirely likely that he would never have got past the professors at the Military College, for he had been in battles but never taken a single course in warfare. He left two daughters; only María Justina, the younger, concerns us here.

In late '53 the colonel's widow and her daughters took up residence in Buenos Aires. They did not recover the place in the country that the tyrant* had confiscated from them, but the memory of those lost leagues of land, which they had never seen, survived in the family for many years. At the age of seventeen María Justina married Dr. Bernardo Jáuregui, who, though a civilian, fought at Pavón and at Cepeda* and died in the exercise of his profession during the yellow fever epidemic.* He left one son and two daughters: Mariano, the firstborn, was a tax inspector whose desire to write the complete biography of the hero (a book he never completed, and perhaps never began to write) led him to frequent the National Library and the Archives. The elder daughter, María Elvira, married her cousin, one Saavedra, who was a clerk in the Ministry of Finance*; the second daughter, Julia, married a Sr. Molinari, who though having an Italian surname was a professor of Latin and a very well-educated man. I pass over grandchildren and great-grandchildren; let it suffice that the reader picture an honest and honorable family of some-what fallen fortune, over which there presides an epic shade and the daughter who was born in exile.

They lived modestly in Palermo, not far from the Guadalupe Church; there, Mariano still recalls having seen, from a trolley car, a lake that was bordered by laborers' and farmers' houses built of unplastered brick rather than sheets of zinc; the poverty of yesterday was less squalid than the poverty we purchase with our industry today. Fortunes were smaller then, as well.

The Rubios' residence was above the neighborhood dry goods store. The stairway at the side of the building was narrow; the railing on the right-hand side continued on to become one side of the dark vestibule, where there were a hall tree and a few chairs. The vestibule opened into the little parlor with its upholstered furnishings, the parlor into the dining room with its mahogany table and chairs and its china cabinet. The iron shutters (never opened, for fear of the glare of the sun) admitted a wan half-light. I recall the odor of things locked away. At the rear lay the bedrooms, the bath, a small patio with a washtub, and the maid's room. In the entire house the only books were a volume of Andrade, a monograph by the hero (with handwritten additions), and Montaner y Simón's Hispano-American Dictionary, purchased because it could be paid for in installments and because of the little dictionary stand that came with it. The family lived on a small pension, which always arrived late, and also received rent from a piece of land (the sole remnant of the once-vast cattle ranch) in Lomas de Zamora.

At the date of my story the elderly lady was living with Julia, who had been widowed, and one of Julia's sons. She still abominated Artigas, Rosas, and Urquiza.* World War I, which made her detest Germans (about whom she knew very little), was less real to her than the 1890 Revolution and the charge on Cerro Alto. Since 1932 her mind had been gradually growing dimmer; the best metaphors are the common ones, for they are the only true ones. She was, of course, a Catholic, which did not mean that she believed in a God Who Is Three yet One, or even in the immortality of the soul. She murmured prayers she did not understand and her fingers told her beads. Instead of the Paschal and Three Kings' Day celebrations that were the custom in Argentina, she had come to adopt Christmas, and to drink tea rather than *mate*. The words *Protestant, Jew, Mason, heretic,* and *atheist* were all synonymous to her, and all meaningless. So long as she was able, she spoke not of Spaniards but of Goths, as her parents had. In 1910 she refused to believe that the Infanta, who after all was a princess, spoke, against all one's expectations, like a common Galician and not like an Argentine lady. It was at her son-in-law's wake that she was told this startling news by a rich relative (who had never set foot in the house though the family eagerly looked for mention of her in the social columns of the newspaper). The names the elderly lady called things by were always out of date: she spoke of the Calle de las Artes, the Calle del Temple, the Calle Buen Orden, the Calle de la Piedad, the Dos Calles Largas, the Plaza del Parque, and the Plaza de los Portones. What were affectations in other members of the family (who would say *Easterners* instead of *Uruguayans,** for instance) came naturally to the widow Jáuregui. She never left her house; she may never have suspected that with the years Buenos Aires had grown and changed. One's first memories are the most vivid ones; the city that the elderly lady saw in her mind's eye on the other side of the front door was no doubt a much earlier one than the city that existed at the time they'd had to move toward the outskirts; the oxen of the oxcarts must still have stood at rest in Plaza del Once,* and dead violets still have perfumed the country houses of Barracas.* *All I dream about now is dead men* was one of the last things she was heard to say. She was never stupid, but she had never, so far as I know, enjoyed the pleasures of the intellect; there remained to her the pleasures of memory, and then, forgetfulness. She was always generous. I recall her tranquil blue eyes and her smile. Who can say what tumult of passions (now lost but erstwhile burning brightly) there had been in that old woman who had once been so charming and well favored. Sensitive to plants, whose modest, silent life was so much like her own, she raised begonias in her room and touched the leaves she could not see. Until 1929, when she fell into her reverie, she would tell stories of historical events, but always with the same words and in the same order, as though they were the Paternoster, and I suspect that after a while they no longer corresponded to images in her mind. She had no marked preferences in food. She was, in a word, happy.

Sleeping, as we all know, is the most secret thing we do. We devote one third of our lives to sleep, yet we do not understand it. Some believe it is only an eclipse of wakefulness; others, a more complex state which embraces at once yesterday, the present, and tomorrow; still others see it as an uninterrupted series of dreams. To say that the elderly lady of my story spent ten years in a state of serene chaos is perhaps an error; every moment of those ten years may have been pure present, without past or future. If so, we should not marvel overmuch at that present (which in our own case we count in days and nights and hundreds of pages torn from many calendars, and in anxieties and events)—we voyage through it every morning before we are fully awake and every night before we fall asleep. Twice every day we are that elderly lady.

The Jáureguis lived, as we have seen, in a somewhat equivocal position. They saw themselves as members of the aristocracy, but those who made up that class knew nothing of them; they were the descendants of a national hero, but most textbooks omitted his name. It was true that a street commemorated Colonel Mariano Rubio, but that street, which very few people were familiar with, was lost behind the cemetery on the west side of the city.

The day of her centennial was drawing near. On the tenth, a uniformed soldier appeared with a letter signed by the minister himself, announcing his visit on the fourteenth. The Jáureguis showed the letter to the entire neighborhood, pointing out the engraved letterhead and the minister's personal signature. The journalists who would be writing the newspaper reports then began dropping by. They were given all the facts; it was obvious they'd never in their lives heard of Colonel Rubio. Virtual strangers called on the telephone, hoping the family would invite them to the celebration.

The household labored diligently in preparation for the great day. They waxed the floors, washed the windows, removed the muslin covers from the chandeliers, shined the mahogany, polished the silver in the china cabinet, rearranged the furniture, and opened the piano in the parlor in order to show off the velvet keyboard cover. There was much scurrying about. The only person not involved in the bustle of activity was the elderly lady herself, who appeared not to understand what was going on. She would smile; Julia, with the help of the maid, dressed her smartly and arranged her hair, as though she were already dead. The first thing visitors would see when they came in the door was the oil portrait of the hero, and then, a little lower and to the right, the sword of his many battles. Even in the most penurious times, the family had refused to sell it; they planned to donate it to the Museum of History. A neighbor very thoughtfully lent them a pot of geraniums for the occasion.

The party was to begin at seven. The invitations gave the hour as six-thirty because the family knew everyone would come a little late, so as not to be the first to arrive. At seven-ten not a soul had come; somewhat acrimoniously, the family discussed the advantages and disadvantages of tardiness: Elvira, who prided herself on her punctuality, declared it was an unforgivable discourtesy to leave people waiting; Julia, repeating the words of her late husband, replied that visitors who arrived late showed their consideration, since if everyone arrives a little late it's more comfortable all around, and no one has to feel rushed. By seven-fifteen not another soul could squeeze into the house. The entire neighborhood could see and envy Sra. Figueroa's car and driver* (or *chauffeur*, as she was heard to call him); she almost never invited the sisters to her house, but they greeted her effusively, so nobody would suspect that they saw each other only once in a blue moon. The president sent his aide-de-camp, a very charming gentleman who said it was an honor to shake the hand of the daughter of the hero of Cerro Alto. The minister, who had to leave early, read a most high-sounding speech filled with excellent epigrams, in which, however, he spoke more of San Martín than of Colonel Rubio. The elderly lady sat in her chair amid the cushions, and at times her head would nod or she would drop her fan. A group of distinguished females, the Ladies of the Nation, sang the national anthem to her, though she seemed not to hear. Photographers arranged the guests into artistic groupings, and their flashbulbs dazzled the celebrants' eyes. There were not enough little glasses of port and sherry to go around. Several bottles of champagne were uncorked. The elderly lady spoke not a single word; she may not have known who she was. From that night onward she was bedridden.

When the strangers had left, the family improvised a little cold supper. The smell of tobacco and coffee had already dissipated the light odor of benzoin.*

The morning and evening newspapers told loyal untruths; they exclaimed upon the almost miraculous memory of the hero's daughter, who was "an eloquent archive of one hundred years of Argentine history." Julia tried to show her those reports. In the dim light, the elderly lady lay unmoving, her eyes closed. She did not have a fever; the doctor examined her and said everything was all right. In a few days she died. The storming of her house by the mob, the unwonted stir, the flashbulbs, the speech, the uniforms, the repeated handshakes, and the popping of the champagne corks had hastened her end. Perhaps she thought it was one of Rosas' posses* that had come.

I think about the men killed at Cerro Alto, I think about the forgotten men of our continent and Spain who perished under the horses' hooves, and it occurs to me that the last victim of that chaos of lances in Peru was to be, more than a hundred years afterward, an elderly lady in Buenos Aires.

The Duel

For Juan Osvaldo Viviano

It is the sort of story that Henry James (whose writings were first revealed to me by Clara Glencairn de Figueroa,* one of the two protagonists of my story) might not have scorned to use. He would have consecrated more than a hundred tender and ironic pages to it, and would have embellished them with complex and scrupulously ambiguous dialogue; he might well have added a touch of melodrama. The essence of the story would not have been altered by its new setting in London or Boston. But the events in fact took place in Buenos Aires, and there I shall leave them. I shall give just a summary of the case, since the slowness of its pace and the worldliness of the circles in which it occurred are foreign to my own literary habits. Dictating this story is for me a modest, sideline sort of adventure. I should warn the reader that the episodes of the tale are less important than the situation that led to them, and less important, too, than the characters that figure in them.

Clara Glencairn was tall and proud and had fiery red hair. Less intellectual than understanding, she was not clever yet she was able to appreciate the cleverness of others—even of other women. In her soul, there was room for hospitality. She was delighted by differences; perhaps that is why she traveled so much. She knew that the locale in which chance set her was a sometimes arbitrary conjunction of rites and ceremonies, yet she found those rituals amusing, and she carried them out with grace and dignity. Her parents, the Glencairns, married her off when she was still quite young to a Dr. Isidro Figueroa—at that time the Argentine ambassador to Canada, though he eventually resigned his post, declaring that in an age of telegrams and telephones, embassies were an anachronism and an unnecessary expense to the nation. That decision earned him the resentment of all his colleagues; though Clara herself liked Ottawa's climate (she was, after all, of Scottish descent) and did not find the duties of an ambassador's wife distasteful, she never dreamed of protesting. Dr. Figueroa died a short time later; Clara, after a few years of indecision and quiet casting about, decided to become a painter. She was inspired to this, perhaps, by her friend Marta Pizarro.

It is typical of Marta Pizarro that whenever she was mentioned, she was defined as the sister of the brilliant (married and separated) Nélida Sara.

Before taking up her brushes, Marta had considered the alternative of literature. She could be witty in French, the language her readings generally were drawn from; Spanish for her was no more than a household utensil, much like Guaraní for the ladies of Corrientes province. Newspapers had put the pages of Argentina's own Lugones and the Spaniard Ortega y Gasset into her hands; the style of those masters confirmed her suspicions that the language to which she had been fated was suited less to the expression of thought (or passion) than to prattling vanity. Of music she knew only what any person might know who dutifully attended concerts. She was from the province of San Luis; she began her career with meticulous portraits of Juan Crisóstomo Lafinur* and Colonel Pascual Pringles,* and these were predictably acquired by the Provincial Museum. From the portraiture of local worthies she progressed to that of the old houses of Buenos Aires, whose modest patios she limned with modest colors rather than the stagy garishness that others gave them. Someone (most certainly not Clara Figueroa) remarked that Marta Pizarro's *oeuvre* took for its models the solid works of certain nineteenth-century Genoese bricklayers.* Between Clara Glencairn and

Nélida Sara (who was said to have fancied Dr. Figueroa at one point) there was always a certain rivalry; perhaps the duel was between those two women, and Marta but an instrument.

Everything, as we all know, happens first in other countries and then after a time in Argentina. The sect of painters, today so unfairly forgotten, that was called "concrete" or "abstract" (as though to indicate its contempt for logic and for language) is one of many examples of this phenomenon. The movement argued, I believe, that just as music is allowed to create a world made entirely of sound, so painting, music's sister art, might essay colors and forms that do not reproduce the forms and colors of the objects our eyes see. Lee Kaplan wrote that his canvases, which outraged the *bourgeoisie*, obeyed the biblical stricture, shared with Islam, against human hands' creating images (Gr. *eidōlon*) of living creatures. The iconoclasts, then, he argued, as breakers of the idols, were returning to the true tradition of pictorial art, a tradition which had been perverted by such heretics as Dürer and Rembrandt; Kaplan's detractors accused him of invoking a tradition exemplified by rugs, kaleidoscopes, and neckties. Aesthetic revolutions hold out the temptation of the irresponsible and the easy; Clara Glencairn decided to become an abstract artist. She had always worshiped Turner; she set out to enrich abstract art with her own vague splendors. She labored without haste. She reworked or destroyed several compositions, and in the winter of 1954 she exhibited a series of temperas in a gallery on Calle Suipacha—a gallery whose specialty was art that might be called, as the military metaphor then in fashion had it, "avant-garde." The result was paradoxical: general opinion was kind, but the sect's official organ took a dim view of the paintings' anomalous forms—forms which, while not precisely figurative, nonetheless seemed not content to be austere lines and curves, but instead suggested the tumult of a sunset, a jungle, or the sea. The first to smile, perhaps, was Clara Glencairn. She had set out to be modern, and the moderns rejected her. But painting itself—the act of painting—was much more important to her than any success that might come of it, and so she continued to paint. Far removed from this episode, Painting followed its own course.

The secret duel had now begun. Marta Pizarro was not simply an artist; she was passionately interested in what might not unfairly be called the administrative aspect of art, and she was undersecretary of a group called the Giotto Circle. In mid-1955 she managed things so that Clara, already admitted as a member, was elected to the group's new board of directors. This apparently trivial fact deserves some comment. Marta had supported her friend, yet the unquestionable if mysterious truth is that the person who bestows a favor is somehow superior to the person who receives it.

Then, in 1960 or thereabout, two "world-renowned artists" (if we may be pardoned the cliché) were competing for a single first prize. One of the candidates, the older of the two, had filled solemn canvases with portraits of bloodcurdling gauchos as tall as Norsemen; his rival, the merest youngster, had earned applause and scandal through studied and unwavering incoherence. The jurors, all past the half century mark, feared being thought to be old-fashioned, and so they were inclined to vote for the younger man, whose work, in their heart of hearts, they disliked. After stubborn debate (carried on at first out of courtesy and toward the end out of tedium), they could not come to an agreement. In the course of the third discussion, someone ventured the following:

"I do not think B is a good painter; I honestly don't think he's as good as Mrs. Figueroa."*

"Would you vote for her?" another asked, with a touch of sarcasm.

"I would," replied the first, now irritated.

That same afternoon, the jury voted unanimously to give the prize to Clara Glencairn de Figueroa. She was distinguished, lovable, of impeccable morality, and she tended to give parties, photographed by the most costly magazines, at her country house in Pilar. The celebratory dinner was given (and its costs assumed) by Marta. Clara thanked her with a few well-chosen words; she observed that there was no conflict between the traditional and the new, between order and adventure. Tradition, she said, is itself a centuries-long chain of adventures. The show was attended by numerous luminaries of society, almost all the members of the jury, and one or two painters.

We all think that fate has dealt us a wretched sort of lot in life, and that others must be better. The cult of gauchos and the *Beatus ille* . . . are urban nostalgias; Clara Glencairn and Marta Pizarro, weary of the routines of idleness, yearned for the world of artists—men and women who devoted their lives to the creation of beautiful things. I presume that in the heaven of the Blessèd there are those who believe that the advantages of that locale are much exaggerated by theologians, who have never been there themselves. And perhaps in hell the damned are not always happy.

Two or three years later the First International Congress of Latin American Art took place in the city of Cartagena. Each Latin American republic sent one representative. The theme of the congress was (if we may be pardoned the cliché) of burning interest: Can the artist put aside, ignore, fail to include the autochthonous elements of culture—can the artist leave out the fauna and flora, be insensitive to social issues, not join his or her voice to those who are struggling against U.S. and British imperialism, et cetera, et cetera? Before being ambassador to Canada, Dr. Figueroa had held a diplomatic post in Cartagena; Clara, made more than a little vain by the award that had been granted her, would have liked to return to that city, now as a recognized artist in her own right. But that hope was dashed—the government appointed Marta Pizarro to be the country's representative. Her performance, according to the impartial testimony of the Buenos Aires correspondents, was often brilliant, though not always persuasive.

Life must have its consuming passion. The two women found that passion in painting—or rather, in the relationship that painting forced them into. Clara Glencairn painted against, and in some sense for, Marta Pizarro; each was her rival's judge and solitary audience. In their canvases, which no one any longer looked at, I believe I see (as there inevitably had to be) a reciprocal influence. And we must not forget that the two women loved each other, that in the course of that private duel they acted with perfect loyalty to one another.

It was around this same time that Marta, now no longer so young as before, rejected an offer of marriage; only her battle interested her.

On February 2, 1964, Clara Figueroa suffered a stroke and died. The newspapers printed long obituaries of the sort that are still *de rigueur* in Argentina, wherein the woman is a representative of the species, not an individual. With the exception of an occasional brief mention of her enthusiasm for art and her refined taste, it was her faith, her goodness, her constant and virtually anonymous philanthropy, her patrician lineage (her father, General Glencairn, had fought in the Brazil campaign), and her distinguished place in the highest social circles that were praised. Marta realized that her own life now had no meaning. She had never felt so useless. She recalled the first tentative paintings she had done, now so long ago, and she exhibited in the National Gallery a somber portrait of Clara in the style of the English masters they had both so much admired. Someone said it was her best work. She never painted again.

In that delicate duel (perceived only by those few of us who were intimate friends) there were no defeats or victories, nor even so much as an open clash—no visible circumstances at all, save those I have attempted to record with my respectful pen. Only God (whose æsthetic preferences are unknown to us) can bestow the final palm. The story that moved in darkness ends in darkness.

The Other Duel

One summer evening in Adrogué* many years ago, this story was told to me by Carlos Reyles, the son of the Uruguayan novelist. In my memory this chronicle of a long-held hatred and its tragic end still calls up the medicinal fragrance of the eucalyptus trees and the singing of the birds.

We were talking, as we always did, about the interwoven history of our two countries. At one point he said I'd surely heard of Juan Patricio Nolan, who had earned a reputation as a brave man, a teller of tall tales, and a practical joker. Lying myself, I said I had. Nolan had died in '90 or thereabout, but people still thought of him as a friend. He had his detractors, too, of course, as we all do. Carlos told me one of the many little pranks that Nolan was said to have played. The incident had taken place a short while before the Battle of Manantiales*; its protagonists were Manuel Cardoso and Carmen Silveira, two gauchos from Cerro Largo.*

How and why had the hatred between those two men begun? How, a century or more later, can we recover the shadowy story of those two men whose only fame was earned in their final duel? There was a man named Laderecha—an overseer at Reyles' father's ranch, "with a mustache like a tiger's"—who had gleaned from "oral tradition" certain details that I shall recount; I set them down here for what they are worth and with no further assurances as to their veracity, since both forgetfulness and recollection are creative.

Manuel Cardoso's and Carmen Silveira's small ranches bordered one another. As with the origins of other passions, the origins of a hatred are always obscure, but there was talk of a dispute over some unmarked animals, or, alternately, of a bareback horse race during which Silveira, who was the stronger, had bumped Cardoso's horse off the track. Months later, in the town's general store, there had been a long game of two-handed *truco*; Silveira congratulated his opponent on his play to virtually every trick, but he left him at the end without a penny. As he was raking the money into his purse, he thanked Cardoso for the lesson he had given him. It was then, I think, that they almost came to blows. The game had been hard fought; the onlookers (there had been many) had to separate them. On that frontier and at that time, man stood up to man and blade to blade; an unusual feature of this story is, as we will see, that Manuel Cardoso and Carmen Silveira crossed paths up in the mountains twice a day, morning and evening, though they never actually fought until the end. Perhaps their only possession in their coarse primitive lives was their hatred, and therefore they saved it and stored it up. Without suspecting, each of the two became the other's slave.

I have no way of knowing whether the events I am about to narrate are effects or causes.

Cardoso, less out of love than for something to do, took a fancy to a girl who lived nearby, a girl everyone called La Serviliana, and he began to court her; no sooner had Silveira discovered this than he began to court the girl in his own way, and carried her off to his shack. After a few months he threw her out; she got on his nerves. Indignant, the woman sought refuge at Cardoso's place; Cardoso spent one night with her and sent her off at noon. He didn't want the other man's leftovers.

It was at about the same time—a little before or after La Serviliana—that the incident with the sheepdog took place. Silveira was very fond of the dog, and had named it Thirty-three.* It was found dead in a ditch; Silveira always thought he knew who'd poisoned the dog.

In the winter of '70, Aparicio's revolution* caught Cardoso and Silveira drinking in that same general-store-and-bar where they'd played their game of *truco*. A Brazilian soldier with mulatto features, heading up a small band of *montoneros*,* came through the door. He gave the men gathered there a rousing speech; their country needed them, he said—the government's oppression was intolerable. He passed out white badges* to pin on, and at the end of that exordium which they had not understood, he and his platoon impressed them into service—they were not even allowed to say good-bye to their families. Manuel Cardoso and Carmen Silveira accepted their fate; a soldier's life was no harder than a gaucho's. They were used to sleeping in the open with a horse blanket as a mattress and a saddle as a pillow, and for the hand accustomed to killing animals, killing a man was not a great deal different. Their lack of imagination freed them from fear and pity alike, though fear did touch them sometimes, just as the cavalry charged them. (The rattle of stirrups and weapons is one of the things you can always hear when the cavalry rides into the action.) But if a man isn't wounded right away, he thinks himself invulnerable. They did not miss the places they'd been born and raised in. The concept of patriotism was foreign to them; in spite of the insignia worn on the hats, one side was much the same as the other to them. They learned what can be done with the lance. In the course of advances and retreats, they at last came to feel that being comrades allowed them to go on being rivals. They fought shoulder to shoulder yet they never, so far as is known, exchanged a single word.

In the fall of '71, which was a hard time, the end came to the two men.

The engagement, which lasted less than an hour, occurred at a place whose name they never learned—historians assign the names later. On the eve of the battle, Cardoso crawled into the captain's tent and asked him, in a whisper, to save one of the Reds for him if they won the next day—he had never cut anybody's throat,* he said, and he wanted to know what it was like. The captain promised that if he conducted himself like a man, he'd grant him that favor.

The Whites outnumbered the Reds, but the Reds had better weaponry. From the top of a hill they commanded, they rained devastation on the Whites. After two charges that failed to reach the peak, the White captain, gravely wounded, surrendered. There on the field, at his request, his men ended his life.

Then they laid down their arms. Captain Juan Patricio Nolan, commander of the Reds, gave a long-winded and flowery order that all the captives' throats be cut. But he was from Cerro Largo, and not unfamiliar with Silveira and Cardoso's long-standing grudge, so he had them brought to him.

"I know you two can't bear the sight of each other," he said, "and that you've been waiting a long time for the chance to settle scores. So I've got good news for you. Before the sun goes down, you're going to get the chance to show which one of you is the toughest. I'm going to have your throats cut, and then you're going to run a race. Like they say—may the best man win."

The soldier who had brought them took them away.

The news spread quickly through the camp. Nolan had wanted the race to crown that evening's performance, but the prisoners sent a committee to ask him if they couldn't watch it, too, and make bets on the winner. Nolan, a reasonable man, let himself be convinced. The men bet money, riding gear, knives, and horses; their winnings would be turned over to their widows and next of kin when the time came. The day was hot; so everyone could have a siesta, the event was put off till four. (They had a hard time waking Silveira up.) Nolan, typically, kept them all waiting for an hour. He had no doubt been reliving the victory with the other officers; the orderly made the rounds with the *mate.*

On each side of the dusty road, against the tents, the ranks of prisoners sat on the ground and waited, hands tied behind their backs so they'd give nobody any trouble. One would occasionally unburden himself with an oath, another murmur the beginning of the Lord's Prayer; almost all were in a state verging on stupefaction. Naturally, they couldn't smoke. They no longer cared about the race, but they all watched.

"When they slit my throat, they're going to grab me by the hair and pull my head back, too," said one man, as though to ally himself with the centers of attention.

"Yeah, but you'll be along with the herd," replied another.

"Along with you," the first man spit.

A sergeant drew the line across the road with a saber. Silveira's and Cardoso's hands had been untied so they wouldn't have to run off-balance. They stood more than five yards apart. They put their toes against the line; some of the officers called out for them not to let them down—they were counting on them. A great deal of money was riding on each man.

Silveira drew Nigger Nolan, whose grandparents had doubtlessly been slaves of the captain's family, and so bore his name; Cardoso drew the regular executioner, an older man from Corrientes who always patted the condemned man on the back and told him: "Buck up, friend; women suffer more than this when they have a baby."

Their torsos straining forward, the two anxious men did not look at each other.

Nolan gave the signal.

The part Nigger Nolan had been given to play went to his head, and he overacted—he slashed Silveira's throat from ear to ear. The man from Corrientes made do with a neat slice. The blood gushed, though, from both men's throats; they stumbled a few steps and then fell headlong. As he fell, Cardoso stretched out his arms. He had won, but he likely never knew that.

Guayaquil*

Now I shall never see the peak of Higuerota mirrored in the waters of the Golfo Plácido, never make my journey to the Western State, never visit that library (which I, here in Buenos Aires, picture in so many different ways, though it must have its own precise existence, contain its own lengthening shadows) where I was to unriddle the handwriting of Bolívar.

As I reread the foregoing paragraph in order to compose the next one, I am surprised by its tone at once melancholy and pompous. It may be that one cannot speak about that Caribbean republic without echoing, however remotely, the monumental style of its most famous historiographer, Capt. Józef Korzeniowski; but in my case there is another reason—that first paragraph was dictated by the intention, deep within me, to imbue a mildly painful and altogether trivial incident with a tone of pathos. But I will relate what happened with absolute honesty; that, perhaps, will help me understand it. After all, when one confesses to an act, one ceases to be an actor in it and becomes its witness, becomes a man that observes and narrates it and no longer the man that performed it.

The incident happened to me last Friday in this same room I am writing in now, at this same hour of the afternoon (though today is somewhat cooler). I know that we tend to forget unpleasant things; I want to record my conversation with Dr. Eduardo Zimmermann (of our sister university to the south) before it is blurred by forgetfulness. My memory of it now is still quite vivid.

The story can be better understood, perhaps, with a brief recounting of the curious drama surrounding certain letters written by Simón Bolívar, "the Liberator of the Americas." These letters were recently exhumed from the files of the distinguished historian don José Avellanos, whose *Historia de cincuenta años de desgobierno* ["A History of Fifty Years of Misrule"] was itself initially believed lost (under circumstances which no one can fail to be familiar with), then discovered and published in 1939 by his grandson, Dr. Ricardo Avellanos. To judge by references I have gathered from various publications, most of these letters are of no great interest, but there is one, dated from Cartagena on August 13, 1822, in which Bolívar is said to give the details of his famous meeting in Guayaquil with Gen. José de San Martín.* One cannot overstress the value of a document in which Bolívar reveals, even if only partially, what took place at that encounter. Ricardo Avellanos, a staunch opponent of his country's current government, refused to surrender the correspondence to the Academy of History; he offered it, instead, to several Latin American republics. Thanks to the admirable zeal of our ambassador, Dr. Melaza, the government of the Argentine was the first to accept Avellanos' disinterested offer. It was decided that a delegate would be sent to Sulaco, the capital of our neighbor country, to make copies of the letters and publish them here. The chancellor of our university, where I am professor of Latin American history, was so kind as to recommend my name to the minister of education as the person to carry out that mission; I also obtained the more or less unanimous support of the National Academy of History, of which I am a member. Just as the date was set for my interview with the minister, we learned that the University of the South (which I prefer to think was unaware of these decisions) had proposed the name of Dr. Zimmermann.

Dr. Eduardo Zimmermann, as the reader perhaps may know, is a foreign-born historian driven from his homeland by the Third Reich and now an Argentine citizen. Of his professional work (doubtlessly estimable), I know at first hand only an article in vindication of the Semitic republic of Carthage (which posterity has judged through the writings of Roman historians, its enemies) and an essay of sorts which contends that government should function neither visibly nor by appeal to emotion. This hypothesis was thought worthy of refutation by Martin Heidegger, who proved decisively (using photocopies of newspaper headlines) that the modern head of state, far from being anonymous, is in fact the *prōtagōnistēs*, the *khoragos*, the David whose dancing (assisted by the pageantry of the stage, and with unapologetic recourse to the hyperboles of the art of rhetoric) enacts the drama of his people. Heidegger likewise proved that Zimmermann was of Hebrew, not to say Jewish, descent. That article by the venerable existential-ist was the immediate cause of our guest's exodus and subsequent nomadism.

Zimmermann had no doubt come to Buenos Aires in order to meet the minister; the minister's personal suggestion, made to me through the intermediary of a secretary, was that, in order to forestall the unpleasant spectacle of our country's two universities disputing for the one prize, it be myself who spoke to Zimmer-mann, to apprise him of where the matter stood. Naturally, I agreed. When I returned home, I was informed that Dr. Zimmer-mann had phoned to tell me he was coming that evening at six. I live, as most people know, on Calle Chile.* It was exactly six o'clock when the doorbell rang.

With republican simplicity, I opened the door to Dr. Zimmer-mann myself and led him toward my private study. He paused to look at the patio; the black and white tiles, the two magnolia trees, and the wellhead drew his admiration. He was, I think, a bit nervous. There was nothing particularly striking about him; he was a man in his forties with a rather large head. His eyes were hidden by dark glasses, which he would occasionally lay on the table and then put back on again. When we shook hands, I noted with some satisfaction that I was the taller, but I was immediately ashamed of my smugness, since this was not to be a physical or even spiritual duel, but simply a *mise au point*, a "getting down to brass tacks," as some might say, though perhaps a rather uncomfortable one. I am a poor observer, but I do recall what a certain poet once called, with ugliness befitting the thing described, his "inelegant sartorial arrangements." I can still see his bright blue suit, much encumbered with buttons and pockets. His necktie, I noticed, was one of those stage magician's bow ties attached with two plastic clips. He was carrying a leather briefcase that I assumed was full of documents. He wore a well-trimmed, military-style mustache; during the course of our conversation he lighted a cigar, and at that, I felt there were too many things on that face. *Trop meublé*, I said to myself.

The linear nature of language, wherein each word occupies its own place on the page and its own instant in the reader's mind, unduly distorts the things we would make reference to; in addition to the visual trivialities that I have listed, the man gave one the impression of a past dogged by adversity.

On the wall in my office hangs an oval portrait of my great-grandfather, who fought in the wars of independence, and there are one or two glass cases around the room, containing swords, medals, and flags. I showed Zimmermann those old *objets de la gloire* and explained where some of them had come from; he would look at them quickly, like a man performing his duty, and (not without some impertinence, though I believe it was an involuntary and mechanical tic) complete my information. He would say, for example:

"Correct. Battle of Junín. August 6, 1824. Cavalry charge under Juárez."

"Suárez," I corrected.

I suspect that the error was deliberate.

"My first error," he exclaimed, opening his arms in an Oriental gesture, "and assuredly not my last! I live upon texts, and I get hopelessly muddled; in you, however, the fascinating past quite literally lives."

He pronounced the *v* almost as if it were an *f*.

Such fawning did not endear the man to me.

Zimmermann found my books more interesting. His eyes wandered over the titles almost lovingly, and I recall that he said:

"Ah, Schopenhauer, who never believed in history. . . .In Prague I had that same edition, Grisebach's, and I believed that I would grow old in the company of those volumes that were so comfortable in one's hand—but it was History itself, embodied in one senseless man, that drove me from that house and that city. And here I am in the New World, in your lovely home, with you. . . ."

He spoke the language fluently, but not without error; a noticeable German accent coexisted with the lisping *s*'s of the Spanish peninsula.

We had taken a seat by now, and I seized upon those last words in order to get down to our business.

"Here, history is kinder," I said. "I expect to die in this house, where I was born. It was to this house that my great-grandfather, who had been all over the continent, returned when he brought home that sword; it is in this house that I have sat to contemplate the past and write my books. I might almost say that I have never left this library—but now, at last, I am to leave it, to journey across the landscape I have only traveled on maps."

I softened my possible rhetorical excess with a smile.

"Are you referring to a certain Caribbean republic?" Zimmermann asked.

"Quite right," I replied. "I believe that it is to that imminent journey that I owe the honor of your visit."

Trinidad brought in coffee.

"You are surely aware," I went on with slow assurance, "that the minister has entrusted me with the mission of transcribing and writing an introduction to the letters of Bolívar that chance has disinterred from the files of Dr. Avellanos. This mission, with a sort of fortunate fatality, crowns my life's labor, the labor that is somehow in my blood."

It was a relief to me to have said what I had to say. Zimmermann seemed not to have heard me; his eyes were on not my face but the books behind me. He nodded vaguely, and then more emphatically.

"In your blood. You are the true historian. Your family roamed the lands of the Americas and fought great battles, while mine, obscure, was barely emerging from the ghetto. History flows in your veins, as you yourself so eloquently say; all you have to do is listen, attentively, to that occult voice. I, on the other hand, must travel to Sulaco and attempt to decipher stacks and stacks of papers—papers which may finally turn out to be apocryphal. Believe me, professor, when I say I envy you."

I could sense no trace of mockery in those words; they were simply the expression of a will that made the future as irrevocable as the past. Zimmermann's arguments were the least of it, however; the power lay in the man, not in the dialectic. He continued with a pedagogue's deliberateness:

"In all things regarding Bolívar—San Martín, I mean, of course—your own position, my dear professor, is universally acknowledged. *Votre siège est fait.* I have not yet read the letter in question, but it is inevitable, or certainly reasonable, to hypothesize that Bolívar wrote it as self-justification. At any rate, the much-talked-about epistle will reveal to us only what we might call the Bolívar—not San Martín—side of the matter. Once it is published, it will have to be weighed, examined, passed through the critical sieve, as it were, and, if necessary, refuted. There is no one more qualified to hand down that ultimate verdict than yourself, with your magnifying glass. And scalpel! if scientific rigor so requires! Allow me furthermore to add that the name of the person who presents the letter to the world will always remain linked to the letter. There is no way, professor, that such a yoking can be in your interest. The common reader does not readily perceive nuances."

I now realize that our subsequent debate was essentially point-less. Perhaps I even sensed as much then; in order not to face that possibility, I grasped at one thing he had said and asked Zimmermann whether he really believed the letters were apoc-ryphal.

"Even if they were written by Bolívar himself," he replied, "— that does not mean they contain the whole truth. Bolívar may have wished to delude his correspondent, or may simply have been deluding himself. You, a historian, a contemplative, know better than I that the mystery lies within ourselves, and not in words."

The man's grandiloquent generalities irritated me, so I curtly observed that within the Great Enigma that surrounds us, the meeting in Guayaquil, in which Gen. San Martín renounced mere ambition and left the fate of the continent in the hands of Bolívar, is also an enigma worth studying.

"There are so many explanations . . .," Zimmermann replied. "There are those who speculate that San Martín fell into a trap. Others, such as Sarmiento, contend that he was in essence a European soldier, lost on a continent he never understood; others still—Argentines, generally—maintain that he acted out of abne-gation; yet others, out of weariness. There are even those who speak of a secret order from some Masonic lodge."

I remarked that be all that as it might, it would be interesting to recover the precise words spoken between the Protector of Peru and the Liberator of the Americas.

"It is possible," Zimmermann pontificated, "that the words they exchanged were trivial. Two men met in Guayaquil; if one prevailed, it was because he possessed the stronger will, not because of dialectical games. As you see, I have not forgotten my Schopenhauer."

Then, with a smile he added:

"*Words, words, words.* Shakespeare, the unparalleled master of words, held them in contempt. In Guayaquil or in Buenos Aires, or in Prague, they always count for less than people do."

At that moment I felt that something was happening—or rather, that something had already happened. Somehow, we were now different. Twilight was stealing upon the room and I had not lighted the lamps. A little aimlessly I asked:

"You are from Prague, professor?"

"I was from Prague," he answered.

In order to avoid the central subject, I remarked:

"It must be a strange city. I am not familiar with it, but the first book I ever read in German was *The Golem*, by Meyrink."

"That is the only book by Gustav Meyrink that deserves to be remembered," Zimmermann replied. "The others, which are concoctions of bad literature and worse theosophy, one is best not to like. Nevertheless, there is something of Prague's strangeness to be found in that book of dreams dissolving into further dreams. Everything is strange in Prague—or, if you prefer, nothing is strange. Anything can happen. In London one afternoon, I had the same sensation."

"You mentioned will," I replied. "In the *Mabinogion*, you may recall, two kings are playing chess on the summit of a hill, while on the plain below, their armies clash in battle. One of the kings wins the game; at that instant, a horseman rides up with the news that the other king's army has been defeated. The battle of men on the battlefield below was the reflection of the battle on the chessboard."

"Ah, a magical operation," Zimmermann said.

"Or the manifestation," I said, "of one will acting upon two distinct battlegrounds. Another Celtic legend tells of the duel of two famous bards. One, accompanying himself on the harp, sang from the coming of day to the coming of twilight. Then, when the stars or the moon came out, the first bard handed the harp to the second, who laid the instrument aside and rose to his feet. The first singer admitted defeat."

"What erudition! What power of synthesis!" exclaimed Zimmermann. Then, in a calmer voice, he added: "I must confess my ignorance, my lamentable ignorance, of *la matière de Bretaigne.* You, like the day, embrace both East and West, while I hold down my small Carthaginian corner, which I now expand a bit with a tentative step into New World history. But I am a mere plodder."

The servility of the Jew and the servility of the German were in his voice, though I sensed that it cost him nothing to defer to me, even flatter me, given that the victory was his.

He begged me not to concern myself about the arrangements for his trip. ("Negotiatives" was the horrendous word he used.) Then in one motion he extracted from his briefcase a letter addressed to the minister, in which I explained the reasons for my withdrawal and listed the acknowledged virtues of Dr. Zimmermann, and laid in my hand his fountain pen so that I might sign it. When he put the letter away, I could not help seeing in his briefcase his stamped ticket for the Ezeiza-Sulaco flight.

As he was leaving, he paused again before the shelf of Schopenhauer.

"Our teacher, our master—our common master—surmised that no act is unintentional. If you remain in this house, in this elegant patrician house, it is because deep inside, you wish to. I respect your wish, and am grateful."

I received these final alms from Zimmermann without a word.

I went with him to the door.

"Excellent coffee," he said, as we were saying our good-byes.

I reread these disordered pages, which I will soon be consigning to the fire. Our interview had been short.

I sense that now I will write no more. *Mon siège est fait.*

The Gospel According to Mark

The incident took place on the Los Alamos ranch, south of the small town of Junín, in late March of 1928. Its protagonist was a medical student named Baltasar Espinosa.* We might define him for the moment as a Buenos Aires youth much like many others, with no traits worthier of note than the gift for public speaking that had won him more than one prize at the English school in Ramos Mejía* and an almost unlimited goodness. He didn't like to argue; he preferred that his interlocutor rather than he himself be right. And though he found the chance twists and turns of gambling interesting, he was a poor gambler, because he didn't like to win. He was intelligent and open to learning, but he was lazy; at thirty-three he had not yet completed the last requirements for his degree. (The work he still owed, incidentally, was for his favorite class.) His father, like all the gentlemen of his day a freethinker, had instructed Espinosa in the doctrines of Herbert Spencer, but once, before he set off on a trip to Montevideo, his mother had asked him to say the Lord's Prayer every night and make the sign of the cross, and never in all the years that followed did he break that promise. He did not lack courage; one morning, with more indifference than wrath, he had traded two or three blows with some of his classmates that were trying to force him to join a strike at the university. He abounded in debatable habits and opinions, out of a spirit of acquiescence: his country mattered less to him than the danger that people in other countries might think the Argentines still wore feathers; he venerated France but

84

had contempt for the French; he had little respect for Americans but took pride in the fact that there were skyscrapers in Buenos Aires; he thought that the gauchos of the plains were better horsemen than the gauchos of the mountains. When his cousin Daniel invited him to spend the summer at Los Alamos, he immediately accepted—not because he liked the country but out of a natural desire to please, and because he could find no good reason for saying no.

The main house at the ranch was large and a bit run-down; the quarters for the foreman, a man named Gutre, stood nearby. There were three members of the Gutre family: the father, the son (who was singularly rough and unpolished), and a girl of uncertain paternity. They were tall, strong, and bony, with reddish hair and Indian features. They rarely spoke. The foreman's wife had died years before.

In the country, Espinosa came to learn things he hadn't known, had never even suspected; for example, that when you're approaching a house there's no reason to gallop and that nobody goes out on a horse unless there's a job to be done. As the summer wore on, he learned to distinguish birds by their call.

Within a few days, Daniel had to go to Buenos Aires to close a deal on some livestock. At the most, he said, the trip would take a week. Espinosa, who was already a little tired of his cousin's *bonnes fortunes* and his indefatigable interest in the vagaries of men's tailoring, stayed behind on the ranch with his textbooks. The heat was oppressive, and not even nightfall brought relief. Then one morning toward dawn, he was awakened by thunder. Wind lashed the casuarina trees. Espinosa heard the first drops of rain and gave thanks to God. Suddenly the wind blew cold. That afternoon, the Salado overflowed.

The next morning, as he stood on the porch looking out over the flooded plains, Baltasar Espinosa realized that the metaphor equating the pampas with the sea was not, at least that morning, an altogether false one, though Hudson had noted that the sea seems the grander of the two because we view it not from horseback or our own height, but from the deck of a ship. The rain did not let up; the Gutres, helped (or hindered) by the city dweller, saved a good part of the livestock, though many animals were drowned. There were four roads leading to the ranch; all were under water. On the third day, when a leaking roof threatened the foreman's house, Espinosa gave the Gutres a room at the back of the main house, alongside the toolshed. The move brought Espinosa and the Gutres closer, and they began to eat together in the large dining room. Conversation was not easy; the Gutres, who knew so much about things in the country, did not know how to explain them. One night Espinosa asked them if people still remembered anything about the Indian raids, back when the military command for the frontier had been in Junín. They told him they did, but they would have given the same answer if he had asked them about the day Charles I had been beheaded. Espinosa recalled that his father used to say that all the cases of longevity that occur in the country are the result of either poor memory or a vague notion of dates—gauchos quite often know neither the year they were born in nor the name of the man that fathered them.

In the entire house, the only reading material to be found were several copies of a farming magazine, a manual of veterinary medicine, a deluxe edition of the romantic verse drama *Tabaré*, a copy of *The History of the Shorthorn in Argentina*, several erotic and detective stories, and a recent novel that Espinosa had not read— *Don Segundo Sombra*, by Ricardo Güiraldes. In order to put some life into the inevitable after-dinner attempt at conversation, Espinosa read a couple of chapters of the novel* to the Gutres, who did not know how to read or write. Unfortunately, the foreman had been a cattle drover himself, and he could not be interested in the adventures of another such a one. It was easy work, he said; they always carried along a pack mule with everything they might need. If he had not been a cattle drover, he announced, he'd never have seen Lake Gómez, or the Bragado River, or even the Núñez ranch, in Chacabuco. . . .

In the kitchen there was a guitar; before the incident I am narrating, the laborers would sit in a circle and someone would pick up the guitar and strum it, though never managing actually to play it. That was called "giving it a strum."

Espinosa, who was letting his beard grow out, would stop before the mirror to look at his changed face; he smiled to think that he'd soon be boring the fellows in Buenos Aires with his stories about the Salado overrunning its banks. Curiously, he missed places in the city he never went, and would never go: a street corner on Cabrera where a mailbox stood; two cement lions on a porch on Calle Jujuy a few blocks from the Plaza del Once; a tile-floored corner grocery-store-and-bar (whose location he couldn't quite remember). As for his father and his brothers, by now Daniel would have told them that he had been isolated— the word was etymologically precise—by the floodwaters.

Exploring the house still cut off by the high water, he came upon a Bible printed in English. On its last pages the Guthries (for that was their real name) had kept their family history. They had come originally from Inverness and had arrived in the New World—doubtlessly as peasant laborers—in the early nineteenth century; they had intermarried with Indians. The chronicle came to an end in the eighteen-seventies; they no longer knew how to write. Within a few generations they had forgotten their English; by the time Espinosa met them, even Spanish gave them some difficulty. They had no faith, though in their veins, alongside the superstitions of the pampas, there still ran a dim current of the Calvinist's harsh fanaticism. Espinosa mentioned his find to them, but they hardly seemed to hear him.

He leafed through the book, and his fingers opened it to the first verses of the Gospel According to St. Mark. To try his hand at translating, and perhaps to see if they might understand a little of it, he decided that that would be the text he read the Gutres after dinner. He was surprised that they listened first attentively and then with mute fascination. The presence of gold letters on the binding may have given it increased authority. "It's in their blood," he thought. It also occurred to him that throughout history, humankind has told two stories: the story of a lost ship sailing the Mediterranean seas in quest of a beloved isle, and the story of a god who allows himself to be crucified on Golgotha. He recalled his elocution classes in Ramos Mejía, and he rose to his feet to preach the parables.

In the following days, the Gutres would wolf down the spitted beef and canned sardines in order to arrive sooner at the Gospel.

The girl had a little lamb; it was her pet, and she prettied it with a sky blue ribbon. One day it cut itself on a piece of barbed wire; to stanch the blood, the Gutres were about to put spiderwebs on the wound, but Espinosa treated it with pills. The gratitude awakened by that cure amazed him. At first, he had not trusted the Gutres and had hidden away in one of his books the two hundred forty pesos he'd brought; now, with Daniel gone, he had taken the master's place and begun to give timid orders, which were immediately followed. The Gutres would trail him through the rooms and along the hallway, as though they were lost. As he read, he noticed that they would sweep away the crumbs he had left on the table. One afternoon, he surprised them as they were discussing him in brief, respectful words. When he came to the end of the Gospel According to St. Mark, he started to read another of the three remaining gospels, but the father asked him to reread the one he'd just finished, so they could understand it better. Espinosa felt they were like children, who prefer repetition to variety or novelty. One night he dreamed of the Flood (which is not surprising) and was awakened by the hammering of the building of the Ark, but he told himself it was thunder. And in fact the rain, which had let up for a while, had begun again; it was very cold. The Gutres told him the rain had broken through the roof of the toolshed; when they got the beams repaired, they said, they'd show him where. He was no longer a stranger, a foreigner, and they all treated him with respect; he was almost spoiled. None of them liked coffee, but there was always a little cup for him, with spoonfuls of sugar stirred in.

That second storm took place on a Tuesday. Thursday night there was a soft knock on his door; because of his doubts about the Gutres he always locked it. He got up and opened the door; it was the girl. In the darkness he couldn't see her, but he could tell by her footsteps that she was barefoot, and afterward, in the bed, that she was naked—that in fact she had come from the back of the house that way. She did not embrace him, or speak a word; she lay down beside him and she was shivering. It was the first time she had lain with a man. When she left, she did not kiss him; Espinosa realized that he didn't even know her name. Impelled by some sentiment he did not attempt to understand, he swore that when he returned to Buenos Aires, he'd tell no one of the incident.

The next day began like all the others, except that the father spoke to Espinosa to ask whether Christ had allowed himself to be killed in order to save all mankind. Espinosa, who was a freethinker like his father but felt obliged to defend what he had read them, paused.

"Yes," he finally replied. "To save all mankind from hell."

"What *is* hell?" Gutre then asked him.

"A place underground where souls will burn in fire forever."

"And those that drove the nails will also be saved?"

"Yes," replied Espinosa, whose theology was a bit shaky. (He had worried that the foreman wanted to have a word with him about what had happened last night with his daughter.)

After lunch they asked him to read the last chapters again.

Espinosa had a long siesta that afternoon, although it was a light sleep, interrupted by persistent hammering and vague premonitions. Toward evening he got up and went out into the hall.

"The water's going down," he said, as though thinking out loud. "It won't be long now."

"Not long now," repeated Gutre, like an echo.

The three of them had followed him. Kneeling on the floor, they asked his blessing. Then they cursed him, spat on him, and drove him to the back of the house. The girl was weeping. Espinosa realized what awaited him on the other side of the door. When they opened it, he saw the sky. A bird screamed; *it's a goldfinch*, Espinosa thought. There was no roof on the shed; they had torn down the roof beams to build the Cross.

Brodie's Report

Tucked inside a copy, bought for me by my dear friend Paulino Keins, of the first volume of Lane's translation of the *Thousand and One Nights* (*An Arabian Night's Entertainment,* London, 1840), we discovered the manuscript that I now make known to the world. The meticulous penmanship—an art which typewriters are teaching us to forget—suggests that the note was written around that same date. Lane, as we all know, lavished long explanatory notes upon the tales; the margins of this volume had been filled with additions, question marks, and sometimes corrections, all in the same hand as that of the manuscript. From those marginalia, one might almost conclude that the reader of the volume was less interested in Scheherazade's wondrous tales than in the customs of Islam. About David Brodie, whose signature (with its fine artistic flourish) is affixed to the end of the manuscript, I have been able to discover nothing save that he was a Scottish missionary, born in Aberdeen, who preached Christianity throughout central Africa and later in certain parts of the jungles of Brazil, a country to which he was led by his knowledge of Portuguese. I do not know when or where he died. The manuscript has never, so far as I know, been published.

I will reproduce the manuscript and its colorless language verbatim, with no omissions save the occasional verse from the Bible and a curious passage treating the sexual practices of the Yahoo, which Brodie, a good Presbyterian, discreetly entrusted to Latin. The first page of the manuscript is missing.

*

. . . of the region infested by the Apemen is the area wherein one finds the *Mlch*.[1] Lest my readers should forget the bestial nature of this people (and also because, given the absence of vowels in their harsh language, it is impossible to transliterate their name exactly), I will call them Yahoos. The tribe consists, I believe, of no more than seven hundred individuals; this tally includes the *Nr*, who live farther south, in the dense undergrowth of the jungle. The figure I give here is conjectural, since with the exception of the king, queen, and various witch doctors, the Yahoos sleep wherever they may find themselves when night falls, in no fixed place. Marsh fever and the constant incursions of the Apemen have reduced their number. Only a very few have names. To call one another, they fling mud at each other. I have also seen Yahoos fall to the ground and throw themselves about in the dirt in order to call a friend. Physically they are no different from the Kroo, except for their lower forehead and a certain coppery cast that mitigates the blackness of their skin. Their food is fruits, tubers, and reptiles; they drink cat's and bat's milk and they fish with their hands. They hide themselves when they eat, or they close their eyes; all else, they do in plain sight of all, like the Cynic school of philosophers. They devour the raw flesh of their witch doctors and kings in order to assimilate their virtue to themselves. I upbraided them for that custom; they touched their bellies and their mouths, perhaps to indicate that dead men are food as well, or perhaps—but this is no doubt too subtle—to try to make me see that everything we eat becomes, in time, human flesh.

In their wars they use rocks, gathered and kept at hand for that purpose, and magical imprecations. They walk about naked; the arts of clothing and tattooing are unknown to them.

I find it worthy of note that while they have at their disposal a broad expanse of grassy tableland, with springs of fresh water

---

1. The *ch* here has the sound of the *ch* in the word *loch*. [Author's note.]

and shady trees, they have chosen to huddle together in the swamps that surround the base of the plateau, as though delighting in the rigors of squalor and equatorial sun. Furthermore, the sides of the plateau are rugged, and would serve as a wall against the Apemen. In the Scottish Highlands, clans build their castles on the summit of a hill; I told the witch doctors of this custom, suggesting it as a model that they might follow, but it was to no avail. They did, however, allow me to erect a cabin for myself up on the tableland, where the night breeze is cooler.

The tribe is ruled over by a king whose power is absolute, but I suspect that it is the four witch doctors who assist the king and who in fact elected him that actually rule. Each male child born is subjected to careful examination; if certain stigmata (which have not been revealed to me) are seen, the boy becomes king of the Yahoos. Immediately upon his elevation he is gelded, blinded with a fiery stick, and his hands and feet are cut off, so that the world will not distract him from wisdom. He is confined within a cavern, whose name is Citadel (*Qzr*)*; the only persons who may enter are the four witch doctors and a pair of female slaves who serve the king and smear his body with dung. If there is a war, the witch doctors take him from the cavern, exhibit him to the tribe to spur the warriors' courage, sling him over their shoulders, and carry him as though a banner or a talisman into the fiercest part of the battle. When this occurs, the king generally dies within seconds under the stones hurled at him by the Apemen.

In another such citadel lives the queen, who is not permitted to see her king. The queen of the Yahoos was kind enough to receive me; she was young, of a cheerful disposition, and, insofar as her race allows, well favored. Bracelets made of metal and ivory and necklaces strung with teeth adorned her nakedness. She looked at me, smelled me, and touched me, and then—in full sight of her attendants—she offered herself to me. My cloth and my habits caused me to decline that honor, which is one granted generally to the witch doctors and to the slave hunters (usually

Muslims) whose caravans pass through the kingdom. She pricked me two or three times with a long golden needle; these pricks are the royal marks of favor, and not a few Yahoos inflict them upon themselves in order to make it appear that they have been recipients of the queen's attentions. The ornaments which I have mentioned come from other regions: the Yahoos believe them to be objects that occur in nature, as they themselves are incapable of manufacturing even the simplest item. In the eyes of the tribe, my cabin was a tree, even though many of them watched me build it, and even aided me. Among other items, I had with me a watch, a pith helmet, a compass, and a Bible; the Yahoos would look at these objects and heft them and ask where I had found them. They would often grasp my hunting knife by the blade; one supposes they saw it differently than I. It is difficult to imagine what they would make of a chair. A house of several rooms would be for them a labyrinth, though they well might not get lost inside it, much as a cat is able to find its way about a house though it cannot conceive it. They all found my beard, which was at that time flaming red, a thing of wonder; they would stroke and caress it for long periods at a time.

The Yahoos are insensitive to pain and pleasure, with the exception of the pleasure they derive from raw and rancid meat and noxious-smelling things. Their lack of imagination makes them cruel.

I have spoken of the king and queen; I will now say something about the witch doctors. I have mentioned that there are four of them; this number is the largest that the Yahoos' arithmetic comprehends. They count on their fingers thus: *one, two, three, four, many*; infinity begins at the thumb. The same phenomenon may be seen, I am told, among the tribes that harass the region of Buenos-Ayres with their raids and pillaging. In spite of the fact that four is the largest number they possess, the Yahoos are not cheated by the Arabs who traffic with them, for in their exchanges all the goods are divided into lots of one, two, three, or four items, which each person keeps beside himself. The operation is slow, yet it allows no room for error or trickery. Of all the nation of the Yahoos, the witch doctors are the only persons who have truly aroused my interest. The common people say they have the power to transform anyone they please into an ant or a tortoise; one individual who noted my incredulity at this report showed me an anthill, as though that were proof. The Yahoos have no memory, or virtually none; they talk about the damage caused by an invasion of leopards, but they are unsure whether they themselves saw the leopards or whether it was their parents, or whether they might be recounting a dream. The witch doctors do possess some memory, though to only a very small degree; in the afternoon they can recall things that happened that morning or even on the previous evening. They also possess the ability to see the future; they quite calmly and assuredly predict what will happen in ten or fifteen minutes. They may say, for example: *A fly will light on the back of my neck*, or *It won't be long before we hear a bird start singing*. I have witnessed this curious gift hundreds of times, and I have thought about it a great deal. We know that past, present, and future are already, in every smallest detail, in the prophetic memory of God, in His eternity; it is curious, then, that men may look indefinitely into the past but not an instant into the future. If I am able to recall as though it were yesterday that schooner that sailed into port from Norway when I was four years old, why should I be surprised that someone is able to foresee an event that is about to occur? Philosophically speaking, memory is no less marvelous than prophesying the future; tomorrow is closer to us than the crossing of the Red Sea by the Jews, which, nonetheless, we remember.

The tribesmen are forbidden to look at the stars, a privilege reserved for the witch doctors. Each witch doctor has a disciple whom he instructs from childhood in the secret knowledge of the tribe and who succeeds him at his death. Thus there are always four—a number with magical qualities, since it is the highest number the mind of humankind may attain. In their own way, they profess the doctrine of heaven and hell. Both are subterranean. To hell, which is bright and dry, shall go the sick, the old, the mistreated, Apemen, Arabs, and leopards; to heaven, which the Yahoos imagine to be dark and marshlike, shall go the king, the queen, the witch doctors, those who have been happy, hardhearted, and bloodthirsty on earth. They worship a god whose name is Dung; this god they may possibly have conceived in the image of their king, for the god is mutilated, blind, frail, and possesses unlimited power. It often assumes the body of an ant or a serpent.

No one should be surprised, after reading thus far in my account, that I succeeded in converting not a single Yahoo during the entire period of my residence among them. The phrase *Our Father* disturbed them, since they lack any concept of paternity. They do not understand that an act performed nine months ago may somehow be related to the birth of a child; they cannot conceive a cause so distant and so unlikely. And then again, all women engage in carnal commerce, though not all are mothers.

Their language is complex, and resembles none other that I know. One cannot speak of "parts of speech," as there are no sentences. Each monosyllabic word corresponds to a general idea, which is defined by its context or by facial expressions. The word *nrz*, for example, suggests a dispersion or spots of one kind or another: it may mean the starry sky, a leopard, a flock of birds, smallpox, something splattered with water or mud, the act of scattering, or the flight that follows a defeat. *Hrl*, on the other hand, indicates that which is compact, dense, or tightly squeezed together; it may mean the tribe, the trunk of a tree, a stone, a pile of rocks, the act of piling them up, a meeting of the four witch doctors, sexual congress, or a forest. Pronounced in another way, or with other facial expressions, it may mean the opposite. We should not be overly surprised at this: in our own tongue, the verb *to cleave* means to rend and to adhere. Of course, there are no sentences, even incomplete ones.

The intellectual power of abstraction demanded by such a language suggests to me that the Yahoos, in spite of their barbarity, are not a primitive people but a degenerate one. This conjecture is confirmed by inscriptions which I have discovered up on the tableland. The characters employed in these inscriptions, resembling the runes that our own forebears carved, can no longer be deciphered by the tribe; it is as though the tribe had forgotten the written language and retained only the spoken one.

The tribe's diversions are cat fights (between animals trained for that purpose) and executions. Someone is accused of offending the modesty of the queen or of having eaten within sight of another; there is no testimony from witnesses, no confession, and the king hands down the sentence of guilty. The condemned man is put to torments which I strive not to recall, and then is stoned. The queen has the right to throw the first stone and the last one, which is ordinarily unnecessary. The people applaud her in frenzy, lauding her skill and the beauty of her person and flinging roses and fetid things at her. The queen wordlessly smiles.

Another of the tribe's customs is its poets. It occurs to a man to string together six or seven words, generally enigmatic. He cannot contain himself, and so he shrieks them out as he stands in the center of a circle formed by the witch doctors and the tribesmen lying on the ground. If the poem does not excite the tribe, nothing happens, but if the words of the poet surprise or astound the listeners, everyone moves back from him, in silence, under a holy dread. They feel that he has been touched by the spirit; no one will speak to him or look at him, not even his mother. He is no longer a man, but a god, and anyone may kill him. The new poet, if he is able, seeks refuge in the deserts to the north.

I have already related how I came to the land of the Yahoos. The reader will recall that they surrounded me, that I fired a rifle shot in the air, and that they took the report for some sort of magical thunder. In order to keep that error alive, I made it a

97

point never to walk about armed. But one spring morning just at daybreak, we were suddenly invaded by the Apemen; I ran down from my plateau, weapon in hand, and killed two of those beasts. The rest fled in terror. Bullets, of course, work invisibly. For the first time in my life, I heard myself applauded. It was then, I believe, that the queen received me. The Yahoos' memory is not to be depended upon; that same afternoon I left. My adventures in the jungle are of no concern; I came at last upon a village of black men, who were acquainted with plowing, sowing, and praying, and with whom I could make myself understood in Portuguese. A Romish missionary, Padre Fernandes, took me most hospitably into his cabin and cared for me until I was able to continue my painful journey. At first it caused me some revulsion to see him undisguisedly open his mouth and put food in. I would cover my eyes with my hands, or avert them; in a few days I regained my old custom. I recall with pleasure our debates on theological questions. I could not persuade him to return to the true faith of Jesus.

I am writing this now in Glasgow. I have told of my stay among the Yahoos, but not of its essential horror, which never entirely leaves me, and which visits me in dreams. In the street, I sometimes think I am still among them. The Yahoos, I know, are a barbarous people, perhaps the most barbarous of the earth, but it would be an injustice to overlook certain redeeming traits which they possess. They have institutions, and a king; they speak a language based on abstract concepts; they believe, like the Jews and the Greeks, in the divine origins of poetry; and they sense that the soul survives the death of the body. They affirm the efficacy of punishment and reward. They represent, in a word, culture, just as we do, in spite of our many sins. I do not regret having fought in their ranks against the Apemen. We have the obligation to save them. I hope Her Majesty's government will not turn a deaf ear to the remedy this report has the temerity to suggest.

A Note on the Translation

(from Collected Fictions)

The first known English translation of a work of fiction by the Argentine Jorge Luis Borges appeared in the August 1948 issue of *Ellery Queen's Mystery Magazine*, but although seven or eight more translations appeared in "little magazines" and anthologies during the fifties, and although Borges clearly had his champions in the literary establishment, it was not until 1962, fourteen years after that first appearance, that a book-length collection of fiction appeared in English.

The two volumes of stories that appeared in that *annus mirabilis*—one from Grove Press, edited by Anthony Kerrigan, and the other from New Directions, edited by Donald A. Yates and James E. Irby—caused an impact that was immediate and overwhelming. John Updike, John Barth, Anthony Burgess, and countless other writers and critics have eloquently and emphatically attested to the unsettling yet liberating effect that Jorge Luis Borges' work had on their vision of the way literature was thenceforth to be done. Reading those stories, writers and critics encountered a disturbingly *other* writer (Borges seemed, sometimes, to come from a place even more distant than Argentina, another literary planet), transported into their ken by translations, who took the detective story and turned it into metaphysics, who took fantasy writing and made it, with its questioning and reinventing of everyday reality, central to the craft of fiction. Even as early as 1933, Pierre Drieu La Rochelle, editor of the influential *Nouvelle Revue Française*, returning to France after visiting Argentina, is famously reported to have said, *"Borges vaut le voyage"*; now, thirty years later, readers didn't have to make the long, hard (though deliciously exotic) journey into Spanish—Borges had been brought to them, and indeed he soon was being paraded through England and the United States like one of those New World indigenes taken back, captives, by Columbus or Sir Walter Raleigh, to captivate the Old World's imagination.

But while for many readers of these translations Borges was a new writer appearing as though out of nowhere, the truth was that by the time we were reading Borges for the first time in English, he had been writing for forty years or more, long enough to have become a self-conscious, self-possessed, and self-*critical* master of the craft.

The reader of the forewords to the fictions will note that Borges is forever commenting on the style of the stories or the entire volume, preparing the reader for what is to come stylistically as well as thematically. More than once he draws our attention to the "plain style" of the pieces, in contrast to his earlier "baroque." And he is right: Borges' prose style is characterized by a determined economy of resources in which every word is weighted, every word (every mark of punctuation) "tells." It is a quiet style, whose effects are achieved not with bombast or pomp, but rather with a single exploding word or phrase, dropped almost as though offhandedly into a quiet sentence: "He examined his wounds and saw, without astonishment, that they had healed." This laconic detail ("without astonishment"), coming at the very beginning of "The Circular Ruins," will probably only at the end of the story be recalled by the reader, who will, retrospectively and somewhat abashedly, see that it changes *everything* in the story; it is quintessential Borges.

Quietness, subtlety, a laconic terseness—these are the marks of Borges' style. It is a style that has often been called intellectual, and indeed it is dense with allusion—to literature, to philosophy, to religion or theology, to myth, to the culture and history of

Buenos Aires and Argentina and the Southern Cone of South America, to the other contexts in which his words may have appeared. But it is also a simple style: Borges' sentences are almost invariably classical in their symmetry, in their balance. Borges likes parallelism, chiasmus, subtle repetitions-with-variations; his only indulgence in "shocking" the reader (an effect he repudiated) may be the "Miltonian displacement of adjectives" to which he alludes in his foreword to *The Maker*.

Another clear mark of Borges' prose is its employment of certain words with, or for, their etymological value. Again, this is an adjectival device, and it is perhaps the technique that is most unsettling to the reader. One of the most famous opening lines in Spanish literature is this: *Nadie lo vio desembarcar en la unánime noche*: "No one saw him slip from the boat in the unanimous night." What an odd adjective, "unanimous." It is so odd, in fact, that other translations have not allowed it. But it is just as odd in Spanish, and it clearly responds to Borges' intention, explicitly expressed in such fictions as "The Immortal," to let the Latin root govern the Spanish (and, by extension, English) usage. There is, for instance, a "splendid" woman: Her red hair glows. If the translator strives for similarity of effect in the translation (as I have), then he or she cannot, I think, avoid using this technique—which is a technique that Borges' beloved Emerson and de Quincey and Sir Thomas Browne also used with great virtuosity.

Borges himself was a translator of some note, and in addition to the translations per se that he left to Spanish culture—a number of German lyrics, Faulkner, Woolf, Whitman, Melville, Carlyle, Swedenborg, and others—he left at least three essays on the act of translation itself. Two of these, I have found, are extraordinarily liberating to the translator. In "Versions of Homer" ("Las versiones homéricas," 1932), Borges makes it unmistakably clear that every translation is a "version"—not *the* translation of Homer (or any other author) but *a* translation, one in a never-ending series, at least an infinite *possible* series. The very idea of *the* (definitive) translation is misguided, Borges tells us; there are only drafts, approximations—*versions*, as he insists on calling them. He chides us: "The concept of 'definitive text' is appealed to only by religion, or by weariness." Borges makes the point even more emphatically in his later essay "The Translators of the 1001 Nights" ("Los traductores de las *1001 Noches*," 1935).

If my count is correct, at least seventeen translators have preceded me in translating one or more of the fictions of Jorge Luis Borges. In most translator's notes, the translator would feel obliged to justify his or her new translation of a classic, to tell the potential reader of this new *version* that the shortcomings and errors of those seventeen or so prior translations have been met and conquered, as though they were enemies. Borges has tried in his essays to teach us, however, that we should not translate "against" our predecessors; a new translation is always justified by the new voice given the old work, by the new life in a new land that the translation confers on it, by the "shock of the new" that both old and new readers will experience from this inevitably new (or renewed) work. What Borges teaches is that we should simply commend the translation to the reader, with the hope that the reader will find in it a literary experience that is rich and moving. I have listened to Borges' advice as I have listened to Borges' fictions, and I—like the translators who have preceded me—have rendered Borges in the style that I hear when I listen to him. I think that the reader of my version will hear something of the genius of his storytelling and his style. For those who wish to read Borges as Borges wrote Borges, there is always *le voyage à l'espagnol.*

The text that the Borges estate specified to be used for this new translation is the three-volume *Obras completas*, published by Emecé Editores in 1989.

In producing this translation, it has not been our intention to produce an annotated or scholarly edition of Borges, but rather a "reader's edition." Thus, bibliographical information (which is often confused or terribly complex even in the most reliable of cases) has not been included except in a couple of clear instances, nor have we taken variants into account in any way; the Borges Foundation is reported to be working on a fully annotated, bibliographically reasoned variorum, and scholars of course can go to the several bibliographies and many other references that now exist. I have, however, tried to provide the Anglophone reader with at least a modicum of the general knowledge of the history, literature, and culture of Argentina and the Southern Cone of South America that a Hispanophone reader of the fictions, growing up in that culture, would inevitably have. To that end, asterisks have been inserted into the text of the fictions, tied to corresponding notes at the back of the book. (The notes often cite sources where interested readers can find further information.)

One particularly thorny translation decision that had to be made involved *A Universal History of Iniquity*. This volume is purportedly a series of biographies of reprehensible evildoers, and as biography, the book might be expected to rely greatly upon "sources" of one sort or another—as indeed Borges' "Index of Sources" seems to imply. In his preface to the 1954 reprinting of the volume, however, Borges acknowledges the "fictive" nature of his stories: This is a case, he says, of "changing and distorting (sometimes without æsthetic justification) the stories of other men" to produce a work singularly his own. This sui generis use of sources, most of which were in English, presents the translator with something of a challenge: to translate Borges even while Borges is cribbing from, translating, and "changing and distorting" other writers' stories. The method I have chosen to employ is to go to the sources Borges names, to see the ground upon which those changes and distortions were wrought; where Borges is clearly translating phrases, sentences, or even larger pieces of text, I have used the English of the original source. Thus, the New York gangsters in "Monk Eastman" speak as Asbury quotes them, not as I might have translated Borges' Spanish into English had I been translating in the usual sense of the word; back-translating Borges' translation did not seem to make much sense. But even while returning to the sources, I have made no attempt, either in the text or in my notes, to "correct" Borges; he has changed names (or their spellings), dates, numbers, locations, etc., as his literary vision led him to, but the tracing of those "deviations" is a matter which the editors and I have decided should be left to critics and scholarly publications.

More often than one would imagine, Borges' characters are murderers, knife fighters, throat slitters, liars, evil or casually violent men and women—and of course many of them "live" in a time different from our own. They sometimes use language that is strong, and that today may well be offensive—words denoting membership in ethnic and racial groups, for example. In the Hispanic culture, however, some of these expressions can be, and often are, used as terms of endearment—*negro/negra* and *chino/china* come at once to mind. (I am not claiming that Argentina is free of bigotry; Borges chronicles that, too.) All this is to explain a decision as to my translation of certain terms—specifically *rusito* (literally "little Russian," but with the force of "Jew," "sheeny"), *pardo/parda* (literally "dark mulatto," "black-skinned"), and *gringo* (meaning Italian immigrants: "wops," etc.)—that Borges uses in his fictions. I have chosen to use the word "sheeny" for *rusito* and the word "wop" for *gringo* because in the stories in which these words appear, there is an intention to be offensive—a *character's* intention, not Borges'. I have also chosen to use the word "nigger" for *pardo/parda*. This decision is taken not without considerable soul-searching, but I feel there is historical justification for it. In the May 20, 1996, edition of *The New Yorker* magazine, p. 63, the respected historian and cultural critic Jonathan Raban noted the existence of a nineteenth-century "Nigger Bob's saloon," where, out on the Western frontier, husbands would await the arrival of the train bringing their wives from the East. Thus, when a character in one of Borges' stories says, "I knew I could count on you, old nigger," one can almost hear the slight tenderness, or respect, in the voice, even if, at the same time, one winces. In my view, it is not the translator's place to (as Borges put it) "soften or mitigate" these words. Therefore, I have translated the epithets with the words I believe would have been used in English—in the United States, say—at the time the stories take place.

The footnotes that appear throughout the text of the stories in the *Collected Fictions* are Borges' own, even when they say "Ed."

This translation commemorates the centenary of Borges' birth in 1899; I wish it also to mark the fiftieth anniversary of the first appearance of Borges in English, in 1948. It is to all translators, then, Borges included, that this translation is—unanimously— dedicated.

Andrew Hurley
San Juan, Puerto Rico
June 1998

Acknowledgments

(from Collected Fictions)

I am indebted to the University of Puerto Rico at Río Piedras for a sabbatical leave that enabled me to begin this project. My thanks to the administration, and to the College of Humanities and the Department of English, for their constant support of my work not only on this project but throughout my twenty-odd years at UPR.

The University of Texas at Austin, Department of Spanish and Portuguese, and its director, Madeline Sutherland-Maier, were most gracious in welcoming the stranger among them. The department sponsored me as a Visiting Scholar with access to all the libraries at UT during my three years in Austin, where most of this translation was produced. My sincerest gratitude is also owed those libraries and their staffs, especially the Perry-Castañeda, the Benson Latin American Collection, and the Humanities Research Center (HRC). Most of the staff, I must abashedly confess, were nameless to me, but one person, Cathy Henderson, has been especially important, as the manuscripts for this project have been incorporated into the Translator Archives in the HRC.

For many reasons this project has been more than usually complex. At Viking Penguin, my editors, Kathryn Court and Michael Millman, have been steadfast, stalwart, and (probably more often than they would have liked) inspired in seeing it through. One could not possibly have had more supportive colleagues, or co-conspirators who stuck by one with any greater solidarity.

Many, many people have given me advice, answered questions,

and offered support of all kinds—they know who they are, and will forgive me, I know, for not mentioning them all personally; I have been asked to keep these acknowledgments brief. But two people, Carter Wheelock and Margaret Sayers Peden, have contributed in an especially important and intimate way, and my gratitude to them cannot go unexpressed here. Carter Wheelock read word by word through an "early-final" draft of the translation, comparing it against the Spanish for omissions, misperceptions and mistranslations, and errors of fact. This translation is the cleaner and more honest for his efforts. Margaret Sayers Peden (a.k.a. Petch), one of the finest translators from Spanish working in the world today, was engaged by the publisher to be an outside editor for this volume. Petch read through the late stages of the translation, comparing it with the Spanish, suggesting changes that ranged from punctuation to "readings." Translators want to translate, *love* to translate; for a translator at the height of her powers to read a translation in this painstaking way and yet, while suggesting changes and improvements, to respect the other translator's work, his approach, his thought processes and creativity—even to applaud the other translator's (very) occasional strokes of brilliance—is to engage in an act of selflessness that is almost superhuman. She made the usual somewhat tedious editing process a joy.

I would never invoke Carter Wheelock's and Petch Peden's readings of the manuscripts of this translation—or those of Michael Millman and the other readers at Viking Penguin—as giving it any authority or credentials or infallibility beyond its fair deserts, but I must say that those readings have given me a security in this translation that I almost surely would not have felt so strongly without them. I am deeply and humbly indebted.

First, last, always, and in number of words inversely proportional to my gratitude—I thank my wife, Isabel Garayta.

Andrew Hurley
San Juan, Puerto Rico
June 1998

Notes to the Fictions

(from Collected Fictions)

These notes are intended only to supply information that a Latin American (and especially Argentine or Uruguayan) reader would have and that would color or determine his or her reading of the stories. Generally, therefore, the notes cover only Argentine history and culture; I have presumed the reader to possess more or less the range of general or world history or culture that JLB makes constant reference to, or to have access to such reference books and other sources as would supply any need there. There is no intention here to produce an "annotated Borges," but rather only to illuminate certain passages that might remain obscure, or even be misunderstood, without that information.

For these notes, I am deeply indebted to *A Dictionary of Borges* by Evelyn Fishburn and Psiche Hughes (London: Duckworth, 1990). Other dictionaries, encyclopedias, reference books, biographies, and works of criticism have been consulted, but none has been as thorough and immediately useful as the *Dictionary of Borges*. In many places, and especially where I quote Fishburn and Hughes directly, I cite their contribution, but I have often paraphrased them without direct attribution; I would not want anyone to think, however, that I am unaware or unappreciative of the use I have made of them. Any errors are my own responsibility, of course, and should not be taken to reflect on them or their work in any way. Another book that has been invaluable is Emir Rodríguez Monegal's *Jorge Luis Borges: A Literary Biography* (New York: Paragon Press, [paper] 1988), now out of print. In the notes, I have cited this work as "Rodríguez Monegal, p. x."

The names of Arab and Persian figures that appear in the stories are taken, in the case of historical persons, from the English transliterations of Philip K. Hitti in his work *History of the Arabs from the Earliest Times to the Present* (New York: Macmillan, 1951). (JLB himself cites Hitti as an authority in this field.) In the case of fictional characters, the translator has used the system of transliteration implicit in Hitti's historical names in comparison with the same names in Spanish transliteration.— *Translator.*

In Praise of Darkness

Foreword

p. 5: *Ascasubi:* Hilario Ascasubi (1807–1875) was a prolific, if not always successful, writer of gaucho poetry and prose. (The *Diccionario Oxford de Literatura Española e Hispano-Americana* gives several titles of little magazines begun by Ascasubi that didn't last beyond the first number.) He was a fervid opponent of the Rosas regime and was jailed for his opposition, escaping in 1832 to Uruguay. There and in Paris he produced most of his work.

Pedro Salvadores

p. 9: *A dictator:* Juan Manuel de Rosas (1793–1877). In Borges, Rosas is variously called "the tyrant" and "the dictator"; as leader of the Federalist party he ruled Argentina under an iron hand for almost two decades, from 1835 to 1852. Thus the "vast shadow," which cast its pall especially over the mostly urban, mostly professional (and generally landowning) members of the Unitarian party, such as, here, Pedro Salvadores. Rosas confiscated lands and property belonging to the Unitarians in order to finance his campaigns and systematically harassed and even assassinated Unitarian party members.

p. 9: *Battle of Monte Caseros:* At this battle, in 1852, Rosas was defeated by forces commanded by Justo José Urquiza, and his tyranny ended.

p. 9: *Unitarian party:* The Unitarian party was a Buenos Aires-based party whose leaders tended to be European-educated liberals who wished to unite Argentina's several regions and economies (the Argentinian Confederation) into a single nation and wished also to unite that new Argentine economy with Europe's, through expanded exports: hence the party's name. The party's color was sky blue; thus the detail, later in the story, of the "sky blue china" in Pedro Salvadores' house.

p. 9: They lived . . . on Calle Suipacha, not far from the corner of Temple: Thus, in what was at this time a northern suburb of Buenos Aires about a mile north of the Plaza de Mayo. This area, later to become the Barrio Norte, was clearly respectable but not yet fashionable (as it was to become after the yellow fever outbreak of 1871 frightened the upper classes out of the area south of the Plaza de Mayo up into the more northern district).

p. 9: The tyrant's posse: The Mazorca (or "corn cob," so called to stress its agrarian rather than urban roots), Rosas' private army, or secret police. The Mazorca was beyond the control of the populace, the army, or any other institution, and it systematically terrorized Argentina during the Rosas years.

p. 10: Smashed all the sky blue china: The color of the china used in the house is the color symbolizing the Unitarian party (see above, note to p. 9) and denounces Salvadores as a follower.

Brodie's Report

Foreword

p. 19: "In the House of Suddhoo": Borges often drops hints as to where one might look to find clues not only to the story or essay in question but also to other stories or essays; he gives signposts to his own "intertextuality." In this case, the reader who looks at this Kipling story will find that there is a character in it named Bhagwan Dass; the name, and to a degree the character, reappear in "Blue Tigers," in the volume *Shakespeare's Memory.*

p. 20: Hormiga Negra: "The Black Ant," a gaucho bandit. Borges includes a note on Hormiga Negra in his essay on *Martín Fierro:* "During the last years of the nineteenth century, Guillermo Hoyo, better known as the 'Black Ant,' a bandit from the department of San Nicolás, fought (according to the testimony of Eduardo Gutiérrez) with bolos [stones tied to the ends of rope] and knife" (*Obras completas en colaboración* [Buenos Aires: Emecé, 1979], p. 546, trans. A.H.).

p. 20: Rosas: Juan Manuel de Rosas (1793–1877), tyrannical ruler of Argentina from 1835 to 1852, was in many ways a typical Latin American caudillo. He was the leader of the Federalist party and allied himself with the gauchos against the "city slickers" of Buenos Aires, whom he harassed and even murdered once he came to power. Other appearances of Rosas may be found in "Pedro Salvadores" (*In Praise of Darkness*) and "The Elderly Lady" (in this volume).

p. 20: And I prefer . . .Here the *Obras completas* seems to have a textual error; the text reads *apto* (adjective: "germane, apt, appropriate") when logic would dictate *opto* (verb: "I prefer, I choose, I opt.").

p. 20: Hugo Ramírez Moroni: JLB was fond of putting real people's names into his fictions; of course, he also put "just names" into his fictions. But into his forewords? Nevertheless, the translator has not been able to discover who this person, if person he be, was.

p. 22: The golden-pink coat of a certain horse famous in our literature: The reference is to the *gauchesco* poem "Fausto" by Estanislao del Campo, which was fiercely criticized by Paul Groussac, among others, though praised by Calixto Oyuela ("never charitable with *gauchesco* writers," in JLB's own words) and others. The color of the hero's horse (it was an *overo rosado*) came in for a great deal of attack; Rafael Hernández, for instance, said such a color had never been found in a fast horse; it would be, he said, "like finding a three-colored cat." Lugones also said this color would be found only on a horse suited for farm work or running chores. (This information from JLB, "La poesía gauchesca," *Discusión* [1932].)

The Interloper

p. 23: 2 Reyes 1:26: This citation corresponds to what in most English Bibles is the Second Book of Samuel (2 Samuel); the first chapter of the "Second Book of Kings" has only eighteen verses, as the reader will note. In the *New Catholic Bible*, however, 1 and 2 Samuel are indexed in the Table of Contents as 1 and 2 Kings, with the King James's 1 and 2 Kings bumped to 3 and 4 Kings. Though my own Spanish-language Bible uses the same divisions as the King James, one presumes that JLB was working from a "Catholic Bible" in Spanish. In a conversation with Norman Thomas di Giovanni, Borges insisted that this was a "prettier" name than "Samuel," so this text respects that sentiment. The text in question reads: "I am distressed for thee, my brother: very pleasant hast thou been unto me: thy love to me was wonderful, passing the love of women." (See Daniel Balderston, "The 'Fecal Dialectic': Homosexual

Panic and the Origin of Writing in Borges," in *¿Entiendes?: Queer Readings, Hispanic Writings*, ed. Emilie L. Bergmann and Paul Julian Smith [Durham: Duke University Press, 1995], pp. 29–45, for an intriguing reading of this story and others.)

p. 24: Those two criollos: There is no good word or short phrase for the Spanish word *criollo*. It is a word that indicates race, and so class; it always indicates a white-skinned person (and therefore presumed to be "superior") born in the New World colonies, and generally, though not always, to parents of Spanish descent (another putative mark of superiority). Here, however, clearly that last characteristic does not apply. JLB is saying with this word that the genetic or cultural roots of these men lie in Europe, and that their family's blood has apparently not mixed with black or Indian blood, and that they are fully naturalized as New Worlders and Argentines. The implicit reference to class (which an Argentine would immediately understand) is openly ironic.

p. 24: Costa Brava: "A small town in the district of Ramallo, a province of Buenos Aires, not to be confused with the island of the same name in the Paraná River, scene of various battles, including a naval defeat of Garibaldi" (Fishburn and Hughes). *Bravo/a* means "tough, mean, angry," etc.; in Spanish, therefore, Borges can say the toughs gave Costa Brava its *name*, while in translation one can only say they gave the town its reputation.

Unworthy

p. 30: The Maldonado: The Maldonado was a stream that formed the northern boundary of the city of Buenos Aires at the turn of the century; the neighborhood around it, Palermo, was known as a rough part of town, and JLB makes reference to it repeatedly in his work. See the story "Juan Muraña," p. 51, for example. Thus, Fischbein and his family lived on the tough outskirts of the city. See also mention of this area on p. 37, below.

p. 31: I had started calling myself Santiago . . . but there was nothing I could do about the Fischbein: The terrible thing here, which most Spanish-language readers would immediately perceive, is that the little red-headed Jewish boy has given himself a saint's name: Santiago is "Saint James," and *as* St. James is the patron saint of Spain, Santiago Matamoros, St. James the Moor Slayer. The boy's perhaps unwitting self-hatred and clearly conscious attempt to "fit in", are implicitly but most efficiently communicated by JLB in these few words.

p. 32: Juan Moreira: A gaucho turned outlaw (1819–1874) who was famous during his lifetime and legendary after death. Like Jesse James and Billy the Kid in the United States, he was seen as a kind of folk hero, handy with (in Moreira's case) a knife, and hunted down and killed by a corrupt police. Like the U.S. outlaws, his fictionalized life, by Eduardo Gutiérrez, was published serially in a widely read magazine, *La Patria Argentina*, and then dramatized, most famously by José de Podestá (for Podestá, see below, in note to "The Encounter," p. 49).

p. 32: Little Sheeny: Fishburn and Hughes gloss this nickname (in Spanish *el rusito*, literally "Little Russian") as being a "slang term for Ashkenazi Jews . . . (as opposed to immigrants from the Middle East, who were known as *turcos*, 'Turks')." An earlier English translation gave this, therefore, as "sheeny," and I follow that solution. The slang used in Buenos Aires for ethnic groups was (and is) of course different from that of the English-speaking world, which leads to a barber of Italian extraction being called, strange to our ears, a gringo in the original Spanish version of the story "Juan Muraña" in this volume.

p. 32: Calle Junín: In Buenos Aires, running from the Plaza del Once to the prosperous northern district of the city; during the early years of the century, a stretch of Junín near the center of the city was the brothel district.

p. 35: Lunfardo: For an explanation of this supposed "thieves' jargon," see the Foreword to this volume, p. 21.

The Story from Rosendo Juárez

p. 36: The corner of Bolívar and Venezuela: Now in the center of the city, near the Plaza de Mayo, and about two blocks from the National Library, where Borges was the director. Thus the narrator ("Borges") is entering a place he would probably have been known to frequent (in "Guayaquil," the narrator says that "everyone knows" that he lives on Calle Chile, which also is but a block or so distant); the impression the man gives, of having been sitting at the table a good while, reinforces the impression that he'd been waiting for "Borges." But this area, some six blocks south of Rivadavia, the street "where the Southside began," also marks more or less the northern boundary of the neighborhood known as San Telmo, where Rosendo Juárez says he himself lives.

p. 36: His neck scarf: Here Rosendo Juárez is wearing the tough guy's equivalent of a tie, the *chalina*, a scarf worn much like an ascot, doubled over, the jacket buttoned up tight to make a large "bloom" under the chin. This garb marks a certain "type" of character.

p. 36: "You've put the story in a novel": Here "the man sitting at the table," Rosendo Juárez, is referring to what was once perhaps JLB's most famous story, "Man on Pink Corner," in *A Universal History of Iniquity*, q.v., though he calls it a novel rather than a story.

p. 37: Neighborhood of the Maldonado: The Maldonado was the creek marking the northern boundary of the city of Buenos Aires around the turn of the century; Rosendo Juárez' words about the creek are true and mark the story as being told many years after the fact. The neighborhood itself would have been Palermo.

p. 39: Calle Cabrera: In Palermo, a street in a rough neighborhood not far from the center of the city.

p. 39: A kid in black that wrote poems: Probably Evaristo Carriego, JLB's neighbor in Palermo who was the first to make poetry about the "riffraff"—the knife fighters and petty toughs—of the slums. JLB wrote a volume of essays dedicated to Carriego.

p. 40: Moreira: See note to "Unworthy," p. 32.

p. 41: Chacarita: one of the city's two large cemeteries; La Recoleta was where the elite buried their dead, so Chacarita was the graveyard of the "commoners."

p. 43: San Telmo: One of the city's oldest districts, it was a famously rough neighborhood by the time of the story's telling. Fishburn and Hughes associate it with a popular song that boasts of its "fighting spirit" and note that the song would have given "an ironic twist to the last sentence of the story."

The Encounter

p. 45: Lunfardo: For an explanation of this supposed "thieves' jargon," see the Foreword to this volume, p. 21.

p. 45: One of those houses on Calle Junín: See note to "Unworthy," p. 32.

p. 46: Moreira: See note to "Unworthy," p. 32.

p. 46: Martín Fierro and Don Segundo Sombra: Unlike the real-life

Juan Moreira, Martín Fierro and Don Segundo Sombra were fictional gauchos. Martín Fierro is the hero of the famous poem of the same name by José Hernández; the poem is centrally important in Argentine literature and often figures in JLB's work, as a reference, as a subject of meditation in essays, or rewritten (in "The End," in the volume *Fictions*, q.v.); his headstrong bravery and antiauthoritarianism are perhaps the traits that were most approved by the "cult of the gaucho" to which JLB alludes here. Don Segundo Sombra is the protagonist of a novel by Ricardo Güiraldes; for this novel, see the note, below, to "The Gospel According to Mark," p. 86. It is interesting that JLB notes that the model for the gaucho shifts from a real-life person to fictional characters, perhaps to indicate that the true gaucho has faded from the Argentine scene and that (in a common Borges trope) all that's left is the memory of the gaucho.

p. 49: The Podestás and the Gutiérrezes: The Podestá family were circus actors; in 1884, some ten years after the outlaw gaucho Juan Moreira's death, Juan de Podestá put on a pantomime version of the life of Moreira. "Two years later," Fishburn and Hughes tell us, "he added extracts from the novel [by Eduardo Gutiérrez] to his performance." The plays were extraordinarily successful. Eduardo Gutiérrez was a prolific and relatively successful, if none too "literary," novelist whose potboilers were published serially in various Argentine magazines. His *Juan Moreira*, however, brought himself and Moreira great fame, and (in the words of the *Diccionario Oxford de Literatura Española e Hispano-Americana*) "created the stereotype of the heroic gaucho." The dictionary goes on to say that "Borges claims that Gutiérrez is much superior to Fenimore Cooper."

Juan Muraña

p. 51: Palermo: A district in Buenos Aires, populated originally by the Italians who immigrated to Argentina in the nineteenth century. Trápani's name marks him as a "native" of that quarter, while Borges and his family moved there probably in search of a less expensive place to live than the central district where they had been living; Borges always mentioned the "shabby genteel" people who lived in that "shabby genteel" neighborhood (Rodríguez Monegal, pp. 48–55).

p. 52: Juan Muraña: As noted in "The Encounter," at one point

Juan Moreira was the very model of the gaucho and therefore of a certain kind of swaggering masculinity; Juan Muraña's name so closely resembles Moreira's that one suspects that JLB is trading on it to create the shade that so literarily haunts this story. In the dream, especially, Muraña has the look of the gaucho: dressed all in black, with long hair and mustache, etc. Nor, one suspects, is it pure coincidence that the story "Juan Muraña" immediately follows the story in which Juan Moreira's ghost plays such a large part.

p. 52: Around the time of the Centennial: The Centennial of the Argentine Declaration of Independence, signed 1810, so the story takes place around 1910.

p. 53: A man named Luchessi: Luchessi's name marks him too as a "native" of Palermo, though he has now moved into a district in southern Buenos Aires, near the bustling (if "somewhat dilapidated" [Fishburn and Hughes]) Plaza de la Constitución and its railway station.

p. 53: Barracas: Fishburn and Hughes gloss this as a "working-class district in southern Buenos Aires near La Boca and Constitución [see note just above] and bordering the Riachuelo."

p. 53: Wop: See note to "Little Sheeny," p. 32, above. In Spanish, *gringo* was the word used to refer to Italian immigrants; see A Note on the Translation.

p. 54: Calle Thames: In Palermo.

The Elderly Lady

p. 57: Wars of independence: For the independence not only of Argentina but of the entire continent. During this period there were many famous generals and leaders, many named in the first pages of this story. Thus Rubio is associated with the grand forces of continental self-determination that battled in the second and third decades of the nineteenth century.

p. 57: Chacabuco, Cancha Rayada, Maipú, Arequipa: Chacabuco (Chile, 1817): The Army of the Andes under General José San Martín fought the Spanish royalist forces under General Marcó del Pont and won. Cancha Rayada (Chile, March 1818): San Martín's army was defeated by the royalists and independence was now very uncertain. Maipú (Chile, April 1818): San Martín's army decisively defeated the royalist forces and secured the independence of Chile. Arequipa (Peru,

1825): General Antonio José de Sucre, leading Bolívar's army, accepted Spain's surrender of the city after a siege; this, after the Battle of Ayacucho (see below), meant the full independence of Peru.

p. 57: He and José de Olavarría exchanged swords: Olavarría (1801–1845) was an Argentine military leader who fought at the battles just mentioned and perhaps at the great Battle of Ayacucho, which determined the full independence of Peru. Exchanging swords was a "romantic custom among generals, and Borges recalls that his own grandfather had exchanged swords with Gen. Mansilla on the eve of a battle" (Fishburn and Hughes). Olavarría and Lavalle (see below) are probably the models for Rubio.

p. 57: The famous battle of Cerro Alto . . . Cerro Bermejo: However famous this battle may be, I confess I have not been able to locate it. I hope (for the good name of the humble research that has gone into these notes) that this is an example of Borges' famous put-ons (see A Note on the Translation). I feel that it may well be; this is the bird's-eye statement given in the *Penguin History of Latin America* (Edwin Williamson, New York/London: Penguin, 1992), p. 228, of the years 1823–1824 as they apply to Bolívar (who is mentioned as winning this battle): "Arriving in Peru in September 1823, Bolívar began to prepare for the final offensive against the royalists. By the middle of 1824 he launched his campaign, winning an important battle at Junín, which opened to him the road to Lima, the ultimate prize. In December, while Bolívar was in Lima, Marshal Sucre defeated Viceroy De la Serna's army at the battle of Ayacucho. Spanish power in America had been decisively broken and the Indies were at last free." Thus, it appears that in April of 1823 Bolívar was planning battles, not fighting them. If it is a real battle, I ask a kind reader to inform me of the date and location so that future editions, should there be any, may profit from the knowledge.

p. 57: Ayacucho: In Peru between Lima and Cuzco (1824). Here Sucre's Peruvian forces decisively defeated the Spanish royalists.

p. 57: Ituzaingó: In the province of Corrientes (1827). Here the Argentine and Uruguayan forces defeated the Brazilians.

p. 57: Carlos María Alvear: Alvear (1789–1852) had led the Argentine revolutionary forces against the Spanish forces in Montevideo in 1814 and defeated them. When he conspired against the Unitarian government, however, he was forced into exile in Uruguay, but was recalled from exile to lead the republican army of Argentina against the Brazilians. He defeated the Brazilians at Ituzaingó, ending the war. He was a diplomat for the Rosas government.

p. 57 Rosas: Juan Manuel de Rosas (1793–1877), tyrannical ruler of Argentina from 1835 to 1852. See note to Foreword, p. 20.

p. 57: Rubio was a Lavalle man: Juan Galo Lavalle (1797–1841), chosen to lead the Unitarians against the Federalists under Rosas, whom Lavalle defeated in 1828. Lavalle was defeated in turn by Rosas in 1829; then "after ten years in Montevideo he returned to lead the Unitarians in another attempt to oust Rosas" (Fishburn and Hughes). Thus he spent his life defending the policies and the principles of the Buenos Aires political party against those of the gaucho party headed by Rosas.

p. 57: The montonero *insurgents:* These were gaucho guerrillas who fought under their local caudillo against the Buenos Aires-based Unitarian forces. While it is claimed that they would have had no particular political leanings, just a sense of resistance to the centralizing tendencies of the Unitarians, the effect would have been that they were in alliance with the Federalists, led by Rosas, etc.

p. 58: Oribe's White army: The White party, or Blancos, was "a Uruguayan political party founded by the followers of Oribe, . . . [consisting] of rich landowners who supported the Federalist policy of Rosas in Buenos Aires. . . .The Blancos are now known as the National-ists and represent the conservative classes" (Fishburn and Hughes). Manuel Oribe (1792–1856) was a hero of the Wars of Independence and fought against the Brazilian invasion of Uruguay. He served as minister of war and the navy under Rivera; then, seeking the presidency for himself, he sought the support of Rosas. Together they attacked Montevideo in a siege that lasted eight days. (This information, Fishburn and Hughes). See also note to p. 70, "Battle of Manantiales," in the story "The Other Duel."

p. 58 The tyrant: Rosas (see various notes above).

p. 58: Pavón and Cepeda: Cepeda (Argentina, 1859) and Pavón (Argentina, 1861) were battles between the Confederation forces under Urquiza and the Buenos Aires-based Porteño forces (basically Unitarian) under Mitre, fought to determine whether Buenos Aires would join the Argentine Confederation or would retain its autonomy. Buenos Aires lost at Cepeda but won at Pavón, enabling Mitre to renegotiate the terms of association between the two entities, with more favorable conditions for Buenos Aires.

   p. 58: Yellow fever epidemic: 1870–1871.

   p. 58: Married . . . one Saavedra, who was a clerk in the Ministry of Finance: Fishburn and Hughes tell us that "employment in the Ministry of Finance is considered prestigious, and consistent with the status of a member of an old and well-established family." They tie "Saavedra" to Cornelio de Saavedra, a leader in the first criollo government of Argentina, in 1810, having deposed the Spanish viceroy. This is a name, then, that would have had resonances among the Argentines similar to a Jefferson, Adams, or Marshall among the Americans, even if the person were not directly mentioned as being associated with one of the founding families. "Saavedra" will also invariably remind the Spanish-language reader of Miguel de Cervantes, whose second (maternal) surname was Saavedra.

   p. 59: She still abominated Artigas, Rosas, and Urquiza: Rosas has appeared in these notes several times. Here he is the archenemy not only of the Buenos Aires Unitarians but of the family as well, because he has confiscated their property and condemned them to "shabby gentility," as Borges would have put it. José Gervasio Artigas (1764–1850) fought against the Spaniards for the liberation of the Americas but was allied with the gauchos and the Federalist party against the Unitarians; in 1815 he defeated the Buenos Aires forces but was later himself defeated by help from Brazil. Justo José Urquiza (1801–1870) was president of the Argentinian Confederation from 1854 to 1860, having long supported the Federalists (and Rosas) against the Unitarians. As a military leader he often fought against the Unitarians, and often defeated them. In addition, he was governor (and caudillo) of Entre Ríos province.

   p. 60: Easterners instead of *Uruguayans:* Before Uruguay became a country in 1828, it was a Spanish colony which, because it lay east of the Uruguay River, was called the Banda Oriental ("eastern shore"). (The Uruguay meets the Paraná to create the huge estuary system called the Río de la Plata, or River Plate; Montevideo is on the eastern bank of this river, Buenos Aires on the west.) *La Banda Oriental* is an old-fashioned name for the country, then, and *orientales* ("Easterners") is the equally old-fashioned name for those who live or were born there. Only the truly "elderly" have a right to use this word.

p. 60: Plaza del Once: Pronounced *óhn-say,* not *wunce.* This is generally called Plaza Once, but the homonymy of the English and Spanish words make it advisable, I think, to modify the name slightly in order to alert the English reader to the Spanish ("eleven"), rather than English ("one time" or "past"), sense of the word. Plaza Once is one of Buenos Aires' oldest squares, "associated in Borges' memory with horse-drawn carts" (Fishburn and Hughes), though later simply a modern square.

p. 60: Barracas: Once a district virtually in the country, inhabited by the city's elite, now a "working-class district" in southern Buenos Aires, near the Plaza Constitución (Fishburn and Hughes).

p. 62: Sra. Figueroa's car and driver: Perhaps the Clara Glencairn de Figueroa of the next story in this volume, "The Duel"; certainly the social sphere in which these two Sras. Figueroa move is the same.

p. 63: Benzoin: Probably used, much as we use aromatic preparations today, to clear the nasal passages and give a certain air of health to the elderly. An aromatic preparation called *alcoholado* (alcohol and bay leaves, basically) is much used in Latin America as a kind of cureall for headaches and various aches and pains and for "refreshing" the head and skin; one presumes this "benzoin" was used similarly.

p. 63: One of Rosas' posses: The Mazorca ("corncob," so called [or so folk etymology has it] for the Federalist party's agrarian ties), a private secret police force-*cum*-army employed by Rosas to intimidate and terrorize the Unitarians after his rise to Federalist power. The Mazorcas beat and murdered many people, and so the elderly lady is right to have been shocked and frightened. (See also the story "Pedro Salvadores" in *In Praise of Darkness.*)

The Duel

p. 64: Clara Glencairn de Figueroa: Clara's name is given here as Christian name + patronymic or family (father's) name + *de* indicating "belonging to" or, less patriarchally, "married to" + the husband's last name. This indication of a character by full name, including married name, underscores Clara's equivocal position in life and in the world of art that she aspires to: a woman of some (limited) talent in her own right, with a "career" or at least a calling in which she is entitled to *personal* respect, versus the "wife of the ambassador." This tension is noted a couple of pages later, when "Mrs." Figueroa, having won a prize, now wants to return to Cartagena "in her own right," not as the ambassador's wife that she had been when she had lived there before. It is hard for the English reader, with our different system of naming, to perceive the subtleties of JLB's use of the conventions of naming in Hispanic cultures.

p. 65: Juan Crisóstomo Lafinur: Lafinur (1797–1824), a great-uncle of Borges', was the holder of the chair of philosophy "at the newly-formed Colegio de la Unión del Sud" (Fishburn and Hughes) and thus a "personage."

p. 65: Colonel Pascual Pringles: Pringles (1795–1831) was a distinguished Unitarian military leader from the province of San Luis. "[R]ather than surrender his sword to the enemy" in defeat, Fishburn and Hughes tell us, "he broke it and threw himself into the river."

p. 65: The solid works of certain nineteenth-century Genoese bricklayers: This snide comment refers to the Italian immigrant laborers and construction foremen who built those "old houses of Buenos Aires" that Marta paints; she is influenced, that is, not by an Italian school of painting (which would be acceptable, as "European" was good; see the first line of the next paragraph in the text) but by Italian immigrant (and therefore, in Buenos Aires society hierarchy, "undesirable" or "inferior") artisans. Note in "The Elderly Lady" the narrator's mild bigotry in the statement that one of the daughters married a "Sr. Molinari, who though of Italian surname was a professor of Latin and a very well-educated man." The social lines between the old criollo families (descendants of European, especially Spanish, colonists), the newer immigrant families, those with black or Indian blood, etc. were clear, especially in the nineteenth century and the early years of the twentieth.

p. 67: Mrs. Figueroa: Here, clear in the Spanish, though difficult to convey in the English, the judge slights Clara Glencairn de Figueroa by referring to her by her married name (Figueroa's *wife*) rather than by her "personal" and "professional" name, Clara Glencairn. She is looked down on, as the story subtly shows, for her social standing, which is in contrast to the *vie bohème* that she would like to think she had lived and the reputation as a painter she would like to think she had earned for herself. Note "Clara Glencairn" throughout the paragraph on p. 66, for the more "professional" or "personally respectful" mode of naming, and note the way the story swings between the two modes as one or another of Clara's "statuses" is being emphasized.

The Other Duel

p. 70: Adrogué: In the early years of the century, a town south of Buenos Aires (now simply a suburb or enclave of the city) where Borges and his family often spent vacations; a place of great nostalgia for Borges.

p. 70: Battle of Manantiales: In Uruguay. For many years (ca. 1837–ca. 1886) Uruguay was torn by rivalry and armed conflicts between the Blancos (the conservative White party) led by, among others, Manuel Oribe and Timoteo Aparicio (see below), and the Colorados (the more liberal Red party) led by Venancio Flores and Lorenzo Batlle. Manantiales (1871) marked the defeat of Aparicio's Blancos by the Colorados under Batlle. Once Cardoso and Silveira are seen joining up with Aparicio's forces, this understated sentence tells the Argentine or Uruguayan reader (or any other Latin American reader familiar, through little more than high school history classes, with the history of the Southern Cone—these dates and places are the very stuff of Latin American history) that their end was fated to be bloody.

p. 70: Cerro Largo: A frontier area in northeast Uruguay, near the Brazilian border. Aparicio had to recruit from all over the countryside, as he was faced by the Triple Alliance of Brazil, Argentina, and the Uruguayan Colorado government.

p. 71: Thirty-three: This in homage to the tiny band of thirty-three soldiers who in 1825 crossed the Uruguay River along with Juan Antonio Lavalleja and Manuel Oribe in order to galvanize the Uruguayans to rise up against the Brazilians who at that time governed them. The flag of the Uruguayan rebellion against Brazil carried the motto *Libertad o Muerte* ("Liberty or Death"). Thus Silveira asserts himself as a tough, independent, and yet "patriotic" gaucho.

p. 72: Aparicio's revolution: See the note to p. 70, above.

p. 72: Montoneros: The *montoneros* were gaucho (Blanco, or White, party) forces, something like quasi-independent armies, organized under local leaders to fight the Unitarians (the Colorados, or Red party) during the civil wars that followed the wars of independence.

p. 72: White badges: To identify them with the Blancos, as opposed to the Colorados (Red party). The armies would have been somewhat ragtag groups, so these badges (or sometimes hatbands) would have been virtually the only way to distinguish ally from enemy in the pitched battles of the civil war.

p. 73: Cut anybody's throat: Here and in many other places in Borges, the slashing of opponents' throats is presented in the most matter-of-fact way. It was a custom of armies on the move not to take prisoners; what would they do with them? So as a matter of course, and following the logic of this type of warfare (however "barbaric" it may seem to us today), losers of battles were summarily executed in this way.

Guayaquil

p. 75: Guayaquil: The name of this city in Ecuador would evoke for the Latin American reader one of the most momentous turns in the wars of independence, since it was here that Generals Simón Bolívar and José San Martín met to decide on a strategy for the final expulsion of the Spaniards from Peru. After this meeting, San Martín left his armies under the command of Bolívar, who went on to defeat the Spaniards, but there is no record of what occurred at the meeting or of the reasons that led San Martín to retire from the command of his own army and leave the glory of liberation to Bolívar. A long historical controversy has been waged over the possible reasons, which the story briefly recounts. Clearly, the "contest of wills" thought by some to have occurred between the two generals is reflected in the contest of wills between the two modern historians. For a fuller (and very comprehensible) summary of this event and the historiographic controversy surrounding it, see Daniel Balderston, *Out of Context: Historical Reference and the Representation of Reality in Borges* (Durham, N.C.: Duke University Press, 1993), pp. 115–131. In this chapter Balderston also discusses Borges' equating of history *with* fiction, providing us another important way of reading the story. See also, for a brief historical summary, *The Penguin History of Latin America* (Edwin Williamson, New York / London: Penguin, 1992), pp. 227–228 and *passim* in that chapter.

p. 76: Gen. José de San Martín: As the note just above indicates, San Martín (1778–1850), an Argentine, was one of the two most important generals of the wars of independence, the other being Simón Bolívar, a Venezuelan. This story is subtly written from the Argentine point of view, because it deals with the reasons—psychological, perhaps, or perhaps military, or, indeed, perhaps other—for which San Martín, after winning extraordinary battles in his own country and in Peru (where he came to be called Protector of Peru), turned his entire army over to Bolívar so that Bolívar could go on to win the independence of the continent from Spain. The enigma of San Martín is one that absorbed the Argentine historical mind for decades, and perhaps still does, so any letters that might have even the slightest, or the most self-serving (if Argentines will forgive me that possible slur on the general's psyche), explanation for his actions would be of supreme importance to Argentine history. This story, then, is filled with those pulls and tugs between one sort of (or nationality of) history and another, one sort of "rationale" and another.

Fishburn and Hughes note that the Masonic lodge mentioned in the story (p.81) is the Logia Lautaro, of which San Martín was indeed a member. Masonic lodges were famed as centers of progressive, not to say revolutionary, thought in the seventeenth and eighteenth centuries. Modern Freemasonry was founded in the seventeenth century.

p.77: Calle Chile: It is Fishburn and Hughes's contention that the physical, geographical location of this street is not really important here, though they give that location as "in the southern part of Buenos Aires, . . . some ten blocks from Plaza Constitución"; their interesting view of this street's mention here is, rather, that it is a symbolic name, linking JLB (that library he had inhabited [see "Juan Muraña" in this volume], the house, and perhaps some of the *objets de la gloire* that JLB had inherited from his grandfather and other members of his family) with the narrator of "Guayaquil": "The narrator lives in a street called Chile, Borges lived in a street called Maipú and both names are associated in the Argentine mind, since San Martín's great victory in Chile was the battle of Maipú."

The Gospel According to Mark

p. 84: Baltasar Espinosa: The Spanish reader will sooner or later associate the young man's surname, Espinosa ("thorny") with the Christian "crown of thorns" evoked at the end of this story.

p. 84: Ramos Mejía: "A part of Buenos Aires in which the rich had weekend houses containing an English colony; now an industrial suburb" (Fishburn and Hughes).

p. 86: A couple of chapters of [Don Segundo Sombra]: The next sentence is perhaps not altogether opaque, but both its sense and its humor are clearer if the reader knows the novel in question. *Don Segundo Sombra* deals with the life of a gaucho (considerably romanticized by nostalgia) and the customs of life on the pampas. Therefore, Gutre *père* sees nothing in it for him; indeed, the *gauchesco* novel was an urban form, a manifestation perhaps of what Marie Antoinette's critics were wont to call *nostalgie de la boue*, or so "The Gospel According to Mark" would seem to imply. JLB himself makes reference to this "urban nostalgia" in the story titled "The Duel," above, on p. 68.

Brodie's Report

p. 93: Qzr: The English reader will not, probably, be able to perceive the fine irony here. Brodie has said that these barbarous people do not have vowels, so he will call them Yahoos. He then gives a few words in their language. Here, the word for "citadel," *qzr*, is the Spanish word for citadel, *alcázar*, with the vowels removed. But the Spanish derives from the Arabic, which does not have vowels; the vowels are sometimes marked, sometimes not; thus, *qzr* is a transliteration of a word that any Spanish speaker would recognize as being fully and legitimately Arabic. Thus the Yahoos are, or might be, Arabs. Here Borges' "traveler's satire" is acute: one can find "barbarism" even in the most refined and advanced of societies; the intolerant eye can see barbarities in others that are invisible in ourselves; "otherness" may itself, to some, be "barbarity."

Collected Fictions
Translated by Andrew Hurley
In intriguing and ingenious fictions, Borges returns again and again to his celebrated themes: dreams, labyrinths, mirrors, infinite libraries, manipulations of chance, knife fighters, tigers, and the elusive nature of identity itself. Playfully experimenting with genres, Borges took the detective story and turned it into metaphysics; made fantasy writing central to the craft of fiction; put the literary essay to use reviewing wholly imaginary books. This edition brings together all of the magical stories, newly rendered in superb translations—both the perfect introduction to the master's work and the perfect one-volume compendium for those who have long loved Borges.

ISBN 0-14-028680-2

Selected Non-Fictions
Edited by Eliot Weinberger
It will surprise some readers that the greater part of Borges's extraordinary writing was not fiction or poetry, but non-fiction prose. Now more than 150 of his most brilliant writings, sure to amaze even aficionados, come together in splendid new translations. Equally at home with Schopenhauer or Ellery Queen, King Kong or the Kabbalists, Lady Murasaki or Hitchcock, Borges's unlimited curiosity and almost superhuman erudition become a vortex for seemingly the entire universe. The first comprehensive selection of this work, *Selected Non-Fictions* presents Borges at once as a deceptively self-effacing guide to the universe and the inventor of a universe that is an indispensable guide to Borges.

Winner of the National Book Critics Circle Award

ISBN 0-14-029011-7

Selected Poems
Edited by Alexander Coleman
This bilingual selection brings together some two hundred poems—the largest collection of Borges's poetry ever assembled in English, including scores of poems never previously translated. Edited by Alexander Coleman, the selection draws from a lifetime's work—from Borges's first published volume of verse, *Fervor de Buenos Aires* (1923), to his final work, *Los conjurados*, published just a year before his death in 1986. Throughout this unique collection the brilliance of the Spanish originals is matched by luminous English versions rendered by a remarkable cast of translators.

ISBN 0-14-058721-7

CLICK ON A CLASSIC
www.penguinclassics.com

The world's greatest literature at your fingertips

Constantly updated information on more than a thousand titles,
from Icelandic sagas to ancient Indian epics, Russian drama to
Italian romance, American greats to African masterpieces

•

The latest news on recent additions to the list, updated
editions, and specially commissioned translations

•

Original essays by leading writers

•

A wealth of background material, including biographies
of every classic author from Aristotle to Zamyatin, plot
synopses, readers' and teachers' guides, useful web links

•

Online desk and examination copy assistance for academics

•

Trivia quizzes, competitions, giveaways, news on
forthcoming screen adaptations